KIDNAPPED!

As Delysia stood looking at her sister's trunk on the pavement, a man's voice behind her suddenly asked:

"Are you Miss Langford?"

She turned her head and saw a man who was obviously a servant.

"Yes, I am Miss Langford," she replied.

Then she gave a frightened scream.

As she spoke, the man had thrown a thick black cloth over her, and a moment later Delysia found herself placed none too carefully on what she was aware was the back seat of a carriage.

Then, as the carriage door was shut, there was the sound of something heavy being dumped overhead, and the horses drove off...

LOVE IS HEAVEN

A Camfield Novel of Love

Camfield Place,
Hatfield
Hertfordshire,
England

Dearest Reader,

Camfield Novels of Love mark a very exciting era of my books with Jove. They already have nearly two hundred of my books which they have had ever since they became my first publisher in America. Now all my original paperback romances in the future will be published by them.

As you already know, Camfield Place in Hertfordshire is my home, which originally existed in 1275, but was rebuilt in 1867 by the grandfather of Beatrix Potter.

It was here in this lovely house, with the best view of the county, that she wrote *The Tale of Peter Rabbit*. Mr. McGregor's garden is exactly as she described it. The door in the wall that the fat little rabbit could not squeeze underneath and the goldfish pool where the white cat sat twitching its tail are still there.

I had Camfield Place blessed when I came here in 1950 and was so happy with my husband until he died, and now with my children and grandchildren, that I know the atmosphere is filled with love and we have all been very lucky.

It is easy here to write of love and I know you will enjoy the Camfield Novels of Love. Their plots are definitely exciting and the covers very romantic. They come to you, like all my books, with love.

Bless you,

Books by Barbara Cartland

A New Camfield Novel of Love by

BARBARA CARTLAND

Love Is Heaven

A JOVE BOOK

LOVE IS HEAVEN

A Jove Book/published by arrangement with
the author

PRINTING HISTORY
Jove edition/January 1985

ISBN: 0-515-08079-9

Jove books are published by The Berkley Publishing Group,
200 Madison Avenue, New York, N.Y. 10016.
The words "A JOVE BOOK" and the "J" with sunburst
are trademarks belonging to Jove Publications, Inc.

PRINTED IN THE UNITED STATES OF AMERICA

Author's Note

Betrothal was in the Seventeenth and Eighteenth Centuries considered as completely binding as the Marriage Ceremony. For a Gentleman to 'cry off' was inconceivable although it occasionally happened. In which case it usually involved a duel with the father or brother of the lady avenging her honour.

Betrothal consisted of the 'interchange of rings—to kiss—the joining of hands—to which was added the testimony of a witness.' In France the presence of a Priest was essential and it was customary in England for the aristocracy to have the engagement printed in *The London Gazette* and later in *The Times* and *The Morning Post*.

Among the ancient Jews betrothal was formal and as binding as marriage. Formal betrothal still retains much of its importance in Europe.

Yet engagements were broken and often elopements took place just before the marriage ceremony. William the Conqueror fell in love with Matilda, a young woman who was promised to someone else. He wooed her roughly—even beating her up—but she fell in love with him and became the first crowned Queen of England.

Chapter One
1824

DELYSIA LANGFORD stepped down from the post chaise which had brought her from the country and could not help looking up somewhat apprehensively at the large, gaunt house which she had not visited for some time.

She was quite certain that she would find a thousand things that needed her attention as soon as she walked through the front door, but for the moment she felt so worn out that all she really wanted to do, was to rest.

She told herself sharply that it was ridiculous to feel like that. She was quite sure that her sister Fleur really needed her, and lacking her supervision the London house would undoubtedly be in a mess.

It was over a year since her father, an outstanding horseman, had had an accident out riding with the result that he had demanded her attention twenty-four hours of the day.

Sir Kendrick Langford was a very intelligent man, an outstanding breeder of horses, and greatly admired in the County where he lived, but no-one, however much they loved him, could say he was a good patient.

The riding accident had resulted in a broken leg, cracked ribs, and a number of other minor injuries which had taken a long time to heal.

Since it had been impossible to get reliable nurses, apart from the village Midwives who kept themselves awake on tots of gin, it had fallen on his elder daughter Delysia to wait on Sir Kendrick hand and foot and to get no thanks for doing so.

As he had to have someone to curse when he was in pain, it was Delysia who heard not only his oaths but his continual complaints that neither she nor the doctors seemed capable of getting him back on his feet.

At the same time Delysia was devoted to her father.

When he was well, she had enjoyed not only riding with him and all the other activities they did together, but also listening to him.

Sir Kendrick was an extremely clever man with considerable knowledge on many varied subjects, and because he had no son, which had been a deep disappointment, he had brought Delysia up as if she were a boy.

He consulted her about his horses and she was ready to ride the wildest of them.

He taught her to shoot and, although she was never allowed to take part in what was essentially a masculine sport when he had guests, they often went out together after partridges, pheasants, pigeons and rabbits, and she had become almost as good a shot as he was.

However, all these activities ceased when Sir Kendrick was laid up, and his demands on Delysia were so excessive that finally the family Doctor had intervened.

"You are better now, Sir Kendrick," he had said firmly, "and I am going to insist that you go to one of the Spas like Cheltenham or Harrogate. That should ensure that the last traces of your injuries disappear under a régime which consists of massage, warm baths, and other treatments which I know you will find beneficial."

Sir Kendrick at first had refused to consider such an idea, but finally had said somewhat grudgingly:

"Perhaps you are right. I do not want to be left crippled for the rest of my life."

"There is no likelihood of that," the Doctor replied. "At the same time you need the right sort of treatment, which you are unable to have here, to put you back in the saddle again."

"Very well, have it your own way," Sir Kendrick replied. "I suppose Delysia will be able to see to it that I do not become too bored surrounded by a lot of invalids."

"Miss Delysia is not going with you."

Sir Kendrick looked at him in astonishment.

"What did you say?"

"I am going to be very frank with you, Sir Kendrick, because I have known you a long time and have not only treated your whole family but respect and admire them all."

He paused and when Sir Kendrick started to speak he interrupted:

"I do not want to have another invalid on my hands, which is inevitable if Miss Delysia does not have a complete rest."

"What are you talking about?" Sir Kendrick growled.

"I am telling you quite frankly that you have overworked your daughter to the point where I am half-afraid she will break down."

"I have never heard such nonsense!"

"Have you any idea how many hours a day she has been waiting on you for over a year?" the Doctor asked. "Sit back and count the times you have had her out of bed this past week."

Sir Kendrick looked guilty and the Doctor persisted.

"When you go to Cheltenham, which I think you will find has better facilities for what you need than anywhere else, I am sending Miss Delysia to London to enjoy herself as she should have been doing instead of acting an an unpaid and unthanked nurse."

Sir Kendrick looked as though he was about to protest but the Doctor added:

"I think also that, while you can now manage very well without Miss Delysia, your other daughter, Miss Fleur, needs her."

Now Sir Kendrick knew exactly what the Doctor was insinuating.

Even in the depths of the country stories about Fleur had come back to them, either from their relatives who called from time to time to see how Sir Kendrick was, or in a more guarded manner from their friends.

"What the devil is Fleur up to?" Sir Kendrick had actually asked Delysia only two days ago.

"I have no idea, Papa. You know she is a very bad letter-writer, and I was thinking only last night that it has been a very long time since she came home."

"Write and tell her I want to see her."

Delysia had agreed that that was what she would do, but when she sat down at her desk and picked up her pen she told herself it was a waste of time.

She knew Fleur was bored by the country and even more bored by her father's illness.

"This place is like a morgue," she had said the last time she had come home. "At least before Papa had his accident there were men dropping in to see him about his horses, or I could ride with him to a Meet and know there would be some congenial company there. But now . . ."

She had finished the sentence with an expressive gesture with her hands and looking at her Delysia could understand that after London she must find the wilds of Buckinghamshire in fact, very boring.

She herself missed the rides she had enjoyed so much, hunting in the winter, and of course her father's many friends.

They had at first made definite efforts to call and enquire after him, but as the months went by the visits got fewer and fewer.

Delysia suspected that when her father did see them they found it not very enlivening to sit by his bedside and listen to his unending grumbling about his injuries.

She knew now that while she had escaped from one problem, thanks to the family Doctor, she was

quite certain that another one in the shape of Fleur
was waiting for her in London.

* * *

It was difficult to imagine that two sisters could be so
different while they each in her own way were very
lovely.

Delysia had a beauty that was not sensational at
first sight, but when people, especially men, first saw
Fleur, they gasped and felt their eyes were deceiving
them, and went on looking until they made sure she
was real.

It was their mother, Lady Langford, who had chosen her daughters' somewhat fantastic names because
they were both so attractive as babies.

"Delysia means 'delightful,'" she had said to her
elder daughter, "and you were not only delightful,
but a delicious baby in every way. I was so thrilled
with you, my dearest, I felt 'Delysia' was just the
right name for you."

"It is rather unusual, Mama, and people look surprised when they hear it."

Lady Langford laughed.

"People like being surprised, and not only has your
father often surprised the social world in which we
live, but so have I!"

That was true, for Lady Langford had been an
acknowledged beauty who had actually been secretly
engaged to a foreign Prince.

He had come to England on a visit and had fallen
head over heels in love with the most beautiful girl
he had ever seen.

6

Whilst negotiations were taking place to make it possible for a foreigner and a member of a European Royal family to take an English bride, she had met Sir Kendrick.

Extremely handsome and dashing, and with a reputation for breaking hearts, he had taken one look at her and she at him, and they had both known there was no-one else of consequence in the whole world.

Because it saved a great deal of disagreeableness and argument they had run away together and been married before anyone realised what was happening and had time to object.

The foreign Prince was desolate. The family of Lady Langford, who had been *persona grata* at Court, were furious at her behaviour and said there could be no good in a young woman who could behave in such an impulsive manner.

Regardless of what everyone said, the Langfords were extremely happy until after fifteen years of what seemed to them sheer bliss, Lady Langford had died whilst having another child which was stillborn.

At first her husband, distraught at losing her, had behaved in such a wild and unconstrained manner that his friends were afraid his brain was affected.

Then strangely enough, he settled down in the country to concentrate on his horses and his two daughters.

It was, however, Delysia who was now fourteen who realised she must look after her father and try to make up to him the loss of her mother.

She also felt she ought to try to mother Fleur, but this was actually much more difficult than coping with her father.

If her mother had been impetuous, impulsive and determined to have her own way, Fleur had the same character but was a thousand times more wilful and, Delysia thought, almost uncontrollable.

All she wanted to do was to enjoy herself, and that meant, even from a very early age, having every man in the vicinity at her feet.

As she was quite the most beautiful girl that had ever been seen in Buckinghamshire, that was not difficult.

Then by the time she was seventeen Fleur was determined to go to London and dazzle the *Beau Ton* of which she had heard a great deal.

The King was growing old, and from all accounts Society was not as gay and amusing as it had been when he was the Regent.

But Fleur had met a few Bucks and Beaux when they came to stay in Buckinghamshire in the few large houses near their own, and they had made sure that the world in which they played a large part was just waiting for her.

It was Fleur who had found Lady Barlow, one of their Langford relations, who was delighted to chaperon her.

Fleur who had arranged without her father and Delysia even being aware of it, that Lady Barlow would present her at Court as soon as the King returned to London.

This ensured that she would be known and noticed, and once that happened she was quite confident of her own success.

Sir Kendrick found it hard to refuse Fleur anything because she looked so like her mother, and gave her, it seemed to Delysia, an astronomical amount of money to spend on clothes.

He conveniently forgot that his elder daughter should have made her début over two years earlier.

"I want you here with me now," he had said, "and later perhaps we will open the house in London."

Delysia had agreed, because she always agreed with what her father asked of her.

She, in fact, was not particularly interested in the social life and did not begrudge or feel the least bit envious of Fleur setting out on what her sister was sure would be a great adventure.

Then three months later, when it had seemed that Sir Kendrick might think of going to London—disaster struck.

After his accident there had been no question of Delysia leaving him, and he even ceased to be interested in learning what Fleur was doing or of the undoubted success she was.

In fact, as she had said to Delysia the last time she had come home:

"I would say I was the Toast of St. James's if it was not a somewhat vulgar thing to be."

"I am so glad, dearest," Delysia replied, thinking that no-one could be lovelier than Fleur with her golden hair, blue eyes, and dazzling complexion.

She was not just a pretty face, she was enticing, entrancing, mischievous and extremely unpredictable.

It was, Delysia thought, inevitable that other women should be jealous of her and, as Fleur said frankly:

"The Dowagers look down their noses at me and label me as fast. Of course I am fast compared to those old snails! I go everywhere, am seen at every party of any importance, and have more Beaux than I can possibly count!"

"Are you thinking of marrying, dearest?" Delysia asked. "After all, you are now eighteen, and perhaps if Mama were here she would think it wise for you to accept one of your many proposals of marriage."

Delysia spoke a little tentatively.

It would be like Fleur to fly at her and say she had no intention of doing anything so boring as getting married when she was having such a fantastic time because she was free.

To her surprise, Fleur rested her pretty, pointed chin on her hands with her elbows on the table and said:

"I have of course considered it, and I was very tempted to accept the Marquess of Gazebrooke when he proposed to me."

"Why did you refuse him?"

"He is nearly fifty and such a pompous bore," Fleur replied. "Also he would have wanted me to live in his big, gloomy mansion in Northumberland and spend my time patting the heads of the tenants and immersed in good works."

Delysia laughed.

"That certainly does not sound like you, at the same time I am sure it would have been a brilliant marriage."

Because Fleur did not answer, after a moment she asked:

"You have not fallen in love?"

"No!" Fleur replied firmly. "The only times my heart gives the slightest flutter, it is always for a man who is penniless and of no importance. I am not such a fool as to accept someone like that."

"At the same time," Delysia replied, "you must remember how Mama and Papa fell headlong in love and how happy they were together."

"I know," Fleur agreed, "but at the same time we are not so stupid, you and I, Delysia, not to know that that was a chance in a million."

She paused before she went on to say:

"In the Social World young women like yourself marry the highest bidder. In other words they choose the man with the most important title and most money. Love, they always say, comes later."

Delysia was shocked.

"Oh, Fleur, I am sure that is wrong, and it is wicked even to think in such a way. Can you imagine Mama being interested in any man except Papa, and he has always said that from the moment he saw her there was no other woman in the whole world but her."

"I know, I know," Fleur agreed crossly, "but those sort of things do not happen today—not to me at any rate."

"Well, what can you do?" Delysia asked a little helplessly.

She felt she was not guiding her younger sister in the way she should.

But because she knew so very little of the London Scene, she felt ignorant and tongue-tied and could only let Fleur talk and listen to what she had to say.

Her sister reeled off a lengthy list of other suitors, and Delysia found herself agreeing that there was something wrong with every one of them.

They were either too old or too young, or extremely unattractive or spendthrifts! She dismissed, the moment she heard about them, those with a bad reputation for women or drink.

"The truth is," Fleur said finally, "I do not believe an ideal man really exists."

"I am sure he does," Delysia agreed, "but you have to wait until you find him."

"As you have already pointed out, I am now eighteen and people are expecting me to be married. Of course, my rivals are praying it will take place as soon as possible so that I will be unable to entice any more men away from them!"

Looking at her sister's lovely face, Delysia was certain that she must be a very real menace to other young women's ambitions.

At the same time, she knew better than anyone else that Fleur would find it hard to settle down with one man unless he was exceptional.

They talked for a long time until Fleur, who had of course, not come home alone but with two young men to escort and amuse her, decided she needed their company.

"We are all returning to London tomorrow morning," she said. "Harry and Willie find this house as gloomy as I do with Papa so ill, and the servants grumbling because there is extra work to do."

Delysia looked guilty.

"Oh, dearest, that is my fault," she cried. "If you had let me know a little earlier that you were coming, I could have arranged for extra help from the village. It is a mistake to have too many servants falling over themselves in the house with nothing to do when Papa is ill. But another time please give me at least twenty-four hours' notice."

Even as she spoke she knew by the expression on her sister's face there might not be another time.

"Please Fleur, come home again soon," she pleaded. "Then you can tell me what you are doing. I am so worried that without Mama you will make mistakes and be sorry for the rest of your life."

"I do not intend to do that," Fleur replied, "and although of course Cousin Sarah is always pressing me to marry a Duke, I want to be happy."

"That is a sensible outlook," Delysia agreed.

At the same time she blamed herself for not having taken more trouble to find the right sort of chaperon for Fleur.

She had actually forgotten that her sister was old enough to begin to chafe at the restrictions she endured in the country, and Delysia thought now that if she had been more aware of what was happening she could have found someone better for Fleur than Lady Barlow.

But she could not put back the clock and the next morning as she watched her sister drive off in a very smart Phaeton with one young man driving and the other riding beside him, she felt as if Fleur was leaving for another planet she would never see.

Yet now, on the Doctor's insistence, she had come to London.

The door was opened by a footman wearing the Langford livery and looking very smart in it.

"Good morning," Delysia said. "I expect Mr. Wrightson told you to expect me."

"Yes, Miss," the footman said, and hurried to the

post-chaise to lift down Delysia's luggage.

Sir Kendrick had said:

"If you are going to London I will not have you sponging on my relatives as Fleur has done this last year. Tell Wrightson to have the house opened and everything ready for you."

"The house? Our own house?" Delysia had asked in surprise. "But there are only the caretakers in charge."

"There are more servants than that," her father replied, "because I told Wrightson that Fleur could go there any time she chose, and some of my friends have used it when they want to stay in London."

"You did not tell me, Papa."

"I suppose I forgot to mention it," her father replied. "They thanked me for my hospitality, so I presume they were comfortable enough."

Delysia was surprised because she had never imagined that the house in London where her father so seldom went, was open.

If she thought of it at all, she envisaged the furniture all shrouded in holland covers, the shutters closed, and only an old couple living in the basement to keep an eye on things.

But now she had the idea that perhaps Fleur had found it convenient to have a house in London at her disposal despite the fact that she was staying with Cousin Sarah.

Mr. Wrightson was not only her father's Solicitor in London but also attended to many of his affairs in the country, that concerned horses or payments.

Delysia had hardly expected him to be waiting for her, and instead the old Butler she remembered came slowly through from behind the staircase shuffling in shoes that had grown too large for him because his feet had shrunk with age.

"It's nice to see you, Miss Delysia," he said in a wheezy voice. "I've been hearing how bad the Master's been and thought you'd never be coming to town."

"I am here now," Delysia smiled. "I hear the house has been open for some time."

"Yes, we've had some good parties here," old Newman replied. "Miss Fleur had a big dinner last week and very pleased she was with everything we done for her."

Delysia was extremely surprised, but did not like to say so.

"Does Miss Fleur know I am arriving today?"

"Yes, Miss. She tells me to say she'd be back about four o'clock."

"Thank you," Delysia replied.

She walked automatically towards the Sitting Room on the ground floor which she thought her father used when he came to London.

"The Drawing Room's open, Miss," Newman said. "Miss Fleur has rearranged the furniture and I'm sure you'll thinks it looks nice."

Bewildered Delysia went up the stairs.

If Fleur was using the house, why had she not written to tell her so?

It seemed extraordinary that she should have given parties on her own when she had always understood that Cousin Sarah was only too delighted to entertain for her at her house in Islington Square.

'I wonder what is going on,' Delysia thought.

As she looked into the Drawing Room she saw that

it was looking very attractive, even though the furniture had been rearranged from the way her mother had had it.

There was too, a profusion of flowers which a quick glance told her had been sent as tributes to her sister.

There were baskets of Orchids, arrangements of Carnations, each with a card on them which obviously carried the name of the sender.

It seemed so strange that they should be sent here, and as a sudden thought struck Delysia she turned to Newman who had come up the stairs behind her.

"Has Miss Fleur been staying here?" she asked.

The old man looked surprised.

"She has been living here, Miss, for the past two months."

"I had no idea," Delysia said. "I thought she was staying with Lady Barlow, but perhaps Her Ladyship has moved here from her own house."

The Butler shook his head.

"No, Miss, I thinks Her Ladyship and Miss Fleur had a bit of a disagreement. Anyhow, Miss Fleur moves in here and says this is hers, she's going to stay."

Delysia gave a little gasp.

"But surely she has a chaperon?"

"Oh, yes, Miss, Lady Matlock is here too."

"I do not think I know her," Delysia said in a low voice.

"Her Ladyship's a widow," Newman said, "and Miss Fleur thought that as she and Her Ladyship are in the main suite, you would like to be in the Rose Room."

It seemed to Delysia extraordinary that her sister should not only be living in the London house without either her father or herself being aware of it, but also that she should be occupying the rooms which were always kept for her father and mother, and not the more simple bedrooms they had used as girls.

She herself had not come up to London very often except, before her mother died, to buy clothes or to visit the dentist.

After her death she had come once with her father to attend a very special sale of horses at which he spent a great deal of money and said very flatteringly that he needed her advice.

She had never at any time anticipated that Fleur would open the London house on her own without even consulting her father and live there with an unknown chaperon who she guessed did not have the approval of Lady Barlow.

She had the feeling she had stepped into a kind of maze when she had least expected it, and it was going to be hard to find her way out.

At the same time she had no wish to discuss her sister's behaviour with one of the servants.

She therefore went to the room that had been chosen for her, and when her luggage was brought upstairs, she changed from her travelling-gown.

She then went to the Drawing Room, realising it was nearly four o'clock and feeling a little apprehensive of what she would learn when Fleur arrived.

She had not long to wait.

Suddenly there was the sound of voices in the hall and the next minute Fleur came into the Drawing

Room looking exquisitely lovely in a gown that was as spectacular as the high-crowned bonnet trimmed with feathers she wore on her golden hair.

"Dearest!" she exclaimed. "How lovely to see you and what a surprise that you should come to London! What have you done with Papa?"

"He has gone to Cheltenham."

"You have not gone with him?"

"Doctor Yates refused to allow me to do so. He said I was worn out looking after Papa, which is more or less true, and that I was to come to London for a rest."

"A rest?" Fleur laughed. "I do not intend to let you have that!"

"Why not?"

"Because, dearest Delysia, now you are here, I will introduce you to the Social World, or rather that part of the Social World over which I reign as an uncrowned Queen."

She spoke in the boastful manner she had used when she was a little girl and was telling Delysia that her doll was bigger and better than hers.

"I do not understand," Delysia said. "Newman tells me you are living here with another chaperon."

Just for a moment her sister looked slightly embarrassed and then she said:

"Cousin Sarah and I fell out."

"What about?"

"What do you think? Men of course."

"I do not understand."

"Do you want the truth?" Fleur said a little defiantly. "She disapproved of a young man I fancied and had the audacity to refuse him the house. So I left."

"Oh, Fleur! How could you do such a thing after she has been so kind?"

"I did not think it kind to interfere with me. So, as I expect Newman has already told you, I have found myself another chaperon."

"But Fleur . . ." Delysia began.

Fleur threw up her hands.

"No, no! Do not start the moment you arrive finding fault with me because I am not going to listen. I have made up my mind to do as I like and to enjoy myself, and I am not going to have anyone, Cousin Sarah or you, telling me what I should or should not do."

"I have no wish to find fault," Delysia said in a soft voice. "It is just rather a surprise, dearest, to find you living here and Papa not to be aware of it."

"I did not ask him because he might have refused," Fleur said with unanswerable logic. "You will find we are very comfortable. I have engaged an excellent chef for my dinner-parties and Newman has two footmen to help him in the Pantry."

"How can you pay for all this?" Delysia asked.

She realised as she asked the question that it was an embarrassing one, and she thought for a moment that Fleur hesitated as if she did not intend to tell her the truth.

She waited a moment and Fleur said:

"My chaperon, Lady Matlock, is very rich and it suited her at this particular moment to be with me."

The way Fleur spoke told Delysia without words

there was some very ulterior motive behind Lady Matlock's action.

But as she tried to form further questions that would not make her seem to be prying, Lady Matlock came into the Drawing Room.

Her first sight of her made Delysia gasp. Never had she imagined anyone could look so exotic, so sensuous, and be almost outrageously attractive.

She held out her hand to Delysia and said:

"I am delighted to meet Fleur's sister, and we are determined to give you, now that you have come to London, a most enjoyable time."

"It is very kind of you," Delysia said.

At the same time she was certain that Lady Matlock was not in the least interested in her, and only accepted her presence among them because Fleur insisted.

They sat down, and as they did so the footman came into the room with tea which he arranged on a table in exactly the same way her mother had always had it.

Delysia saw that the silver had all been brought out of the safe and cleaned, which it had not been the last time she had come to London.

There were a lot of delicious things to eat and she was surprised when Lady Matlock told the footman to bring her a glass of Champagne.

She noticed now that there was a table which had never been there before, at the far end of the room on which there reposed a large number of drinks.

Fleur, Delysia was thankful to find, was quite content with a cup of tea. It seemed to her very strange for any lady, especially one as young as Lady Matlack, to be drinking Champagne so early in the day.

She was, she found, expected to listen wide-eyed while Fleur and Lady Matlock talked of all the things they had been doing in the last twenty-four hours and set out a whole programme of what had been planned for this evening and the next few days ahead.

"Tonight," Fleur said, "we have a special dinner-party and one guest I particularly want you to meet."

"Who is that?" Delysia asked.

She saw her sister glance somewhat knowingly at Lady Matlock before she said:

"Lord Sheldon—Timothy is a very great friend of mine."

The voice in which she spoke, told Delysia, who knew her so well, that Timothy meant something very special that she was sure her sister had not found before.

She did not, however, say anything more about him but went on to describe the other guests.

"Last, but by no means least," Fleur said with another little look at Lady Matlock, "the most distinguished guest here this evening will be the Duke of Hastings."

"If he can get away," Lady Matlock added.

"Of course," Fleur answered, "but I am quite sure he will manage to do so."

"I shall be very angry if anything happens to prevent it," Lady Matlock said.

She put down her empty glass.

"I want to look my best. So I am now going to have a lie-down. My hairdresser will be here at seven, and if you want him, Fleur, he had better come to you first, otherwise you will be late for dinner."

"I will tell the servants to bring him to my room as soon as he arrives," Fleur answered.

Lady Matlock went from the Drawing Room to leave the two sisters alone.

Delysia was just about to ask Fleur to tell her more about Lord Sheldon when Fleur said as if her thoughts were still with Lady Matlock:

"I hope the Duke does not cancel at the last moment. If he does, it will put Beatrice in a rage, and also will make us odd numbers."

"Why should he do that?" Delysia asked.

"It is his tiresome wife," Fleur explained. "She clings to him like a leech, and although he is madly in love with Beatrice he does not particularly want a scandal, not until he has really made up his mind whether he will run away with her or not."

She spoke quite naturally, as if what she was saying was not in the least surprising.

It was only when she heard her sister give an audible gasp and saw Delysia's eyes so wide and astonished that they seemed to fill her whole face, that she realised how shocked she was.

Chapter Two

LOOKING ROUND THE Dining Room, Delysia could understand why Fleur found London very much more exciting than the country.

They were a party of twenty, and when the guests had arrived she was sure it would be impossible anywhere to find more beautiful women gathered in one place or smarter and more distinguished men.

There was no doubt, however, that Fleur outshone them all.

Lady Matlock, in a glittering gown with what Delysia thought an embarrassingly low décolleté, looked as if she should be on the stage rather than in a lady's Drawing Room.

She learnt that Lord Sheldon had been told to bring an extra man for her to make the numbers right.

When this gentleman sat next to her at the table

she could see that everyone else seemed to be paired off with partners with whom they appeared to be very enamoured.

There was no doubt that Lord Sheldon was a very good-looking young man, and it was obvious that he was head-over-heels in love with Fleur.

Delysia, knowing her so well, thought that when she was talking to him, her sister seemed more animated, happier, and certainly more beautiful than she had ever seen her before.

"She is in love," she told herself.

She thought that would make everything easy as Fleur could perhaps be married by the end of the Summer and would not have to come back to the country for the Winter which she would hate.

Sitting there making plans, she jumped when Mr. Hugo Ludgrove, who had been invited on her behalf, said:

"I cannot believe that any family has two lovelier young women in it than yours. If there were a dozen of you it would cause a riot!"

Delysia laughed.

"You are quite safe! Fleur and I have no sisters, or brothers for that matter."

Hugo Ludgrove's eyes went towards Fleur sitting at the end of the table who at that moment, was obviously flirting outrageously with Lord Sheldon.

"Your sister has been a sensation," he said.

"I am glad," Delysia smiled, "and I know she had enjoyed herself in London."

"It is a tragedy however for Timothy."

Delysia did not understand who Timothy was, but Mr. Ludgrove explained that was Lord Sheldon's

Christian name, although most people called him 'Tim.'

"Why is there a tragedy?" Delysia began to ask.

But at that moment Mr. Ludgrove's attention was claimed by the Lady on his other side and she thought he had not heard her.

However, she took the opportunity of looking again at Lord Sheldon, and decided he certainly did not look tragic.

She wondered a little apprehensively if perhaps he had no money, for that would certainly be an impediment if Fleur was wanting to marry him.

The party grew noisier with a great deal of laughter towards the end of dinner.

Afterwards, when the Ladies withdrew into the Drawing Room, they gossiped amongst themselves and Delysia felt rather out of it.

She knew none of the people they were talking about and nobody seemed interested in drawing her into their conversation.

When the Gentlemen joined the Ladies, the Duke of Hastings who had fortunately arrived just in time for dinner, went straight to Lady Matlock's side although he had talked to her all through dinner.

She looked up at him with such an intimate expression on her face that Delysia felt embarrassed.

She was sure that a woman who was having a love-affair with a married man was the last person to be the right chaperon for Fleur.

She wondered how tactfully she could suggest to her sister it would be better either for her to return to Lady Barlow's care or else get someone else to chaperon her.

She was quite certain, without knowing anything about Lady Matlock, that she had a bad reputation.

Looking around the Drawing Room she realised that all the other Ladies in the room, although very beautiful, were much older than Fleur, and she suspected they were all married women.

She began to feel frantically that this was entirely the wrong environment for her sister, who should be with girls of her own age. As it was, she feared that the more respectable hostesses would undoubtedly ostracize her.

Delysia knew very little about the Social World, but her commonsense told her that it was absolutely essential that Fleur did not get a reputation for being, as she had said herself, 'fast.'

'Lady Matlock is fast,' she decided, and although she knew nothing about them, she had an idea that the same could be said about the other Ladies present.

The gentlemen were different.

The majority of them had titles and names that were distinguished.

Since many of them were race-horse owners, she had heard her father speak of them, but now she thought about it, she was almost certain that most of them were also married although they had not brought their wives with them this evening.

Soon after the Gentlemen joined the Ladies, there was a sound of music from a room that adjoined the Drawing Room which had always been called the Library, although there were, in fact, very few books in it.

These had some time previously, been removed to make room for some of her grandmother's furniture and a number of pictures which Delysia could re-member her mother had always thought rather dull, as they were mostly of the Langford ancestors.

As everyone moved towards the sound of music, she found the room had been transformed.

The pictures of the Langfords had vanished and instead the walls were draped with Viennese velvet and garlands of flowers.

It was certainly very attractive and hanging from the centre of the ceiling there was a large chandelier which Delysia did not remember. In an alcove at the end was a small orchestra who were playing a Waltz.

Delysia had heard that the Waltz had been intro-duced by the Princess de Lieven, but she had only seen it danced once rather badly at a Hunt Ball last Winter.

Now under the candlelight it seemed, as the Gentle-men swept the Ladies around the room, they had a grace and elegance which she had not expected.

They had only just started to dance when a number of other guests appeared, all of whom greeted Fleur with cries of delight which seemed to Delysia some-what over-exuberant.

The Gentlemen immediately went to the corner of the room where on a table there was every sort of drink set out, including a number of bottles of Cham-pagne in ice-buckets.

It was all so different from what Delysia had ex-pected in her own home, and she could only stare around in surprise until Mr. Ludgrove was at her side.

"Will you dance with me, lovely Lady?" he asked.

The way he spoke with a slight slur in his speech made Delysia aware that after she had left him in the

Dining Room he must have drunk a great deal more than he had already.

She was aware that during dinner, while the food was excellent and there were many new dishes she had not tasted before, there was also a great deal of drink, far more than her father ever served at home.

There were also many more footmen to fill up the glasses than the two that Fleur had told her were helping old Newman in the Pantry.

"Who can be paying for all this?" Delysia asked herself.

If it was Lady Matlock, as Fleur had hinted, she thought it a mistake to allow her to be a hostess in her father's house without his permission.

She realised now that Mr. Ludgrove was waiting for her reply and she said:

"I am afraid I do not waltz, but perhaps we can sit down and watch the others."

"Good idea," he said in a somewhat thick voice.

As they moved towards some chairs at the side of the room, Delysia was aware that he was walking unsteadily.

They sat down and because she had no wish to be rude to him, she said:

"Would you be very kind and tell me who everyone is? As I have not been in London for years, everyone here, with the exception of my sister, is a stranger."

"You will not be a stranger for long," Mr. Ludgrove replied. "Fleur is the prettiest girl I have ever seen, but you equal her loveliness and I am delighted to be one of the first of a thousand men to tell you so."

It was a pretty speech, unfortunately spoilt by the

fact that he stumbled over some of his words.

"Thank you," Delysia said. "Now tell me who the lady in blue is, who has just gone past us."

He answered her question with a name she had never heard before.

"But then," he continued, "she is in disgrace at the moment having left her children and her husband in the country to come to London, although he had forbidden her to do so."

Delysia drew in her breath, but she did not say anything.

Everything she heard subsequently made her more determined to have a very serious talk with Fleur in the morning.

Because she was tired after her long journey and, as the Doctor had known, worn out from looking after her father she began to find difficulty in keeping her eyes open.

She knew it would be a mistake to draw attention to herself, so she merely waited until Hugo Ludgrove was talking to another man and slipped out of the room.

As she did so she could see more people arriving in the Hall below and was quite certain the party would go on until the early hours of the morning.

She knew, however, that no-one would miss her and she felt that if she did not lie down she would fall down from sheer fatigue.

There was an elderly maid waiting for her in her bedroom and after she had undone her gown Delysia said with a smile:

"I am tired, and I suspect that you must be tired too."

"I am, Miss," the maid answered. "There has been a lot to do these past weeks. Parties, with people to dinner almost every night."

Delysia did not say anything, but when she was alone, instead of sleeping she found herself worrying over Fleur.

How could she be living in this extravagant way with neither her father nor herself being aware of it?

It had only been going on for two months, but even in such a small time she must have spent an enormous amount of money—or Lady Matlock must have done so, which was something which Delysia was sure should not continue.

Then she told herself if Fleur was in love with Lord Sheldon as he was quite obviously in love with her, it would solve every problem.

Then like a buzzing of a mosquito in her mind she remembered Mr. Ludgrove had referred to a tragedy, but what he had meant she had no idea.

What could it be?

Perhaps his father had just died, which would mean he could not be married for a year, although that was not an insurmountable barrier.

Delysia felt her worry lighten a little and she was smiling when she fell asleep.

* * *

The next morning she awoke later than usual and rang the bell for the maid.

When she came after a slight delay she exclaimed: "You are very early, Miss."

"Early?" Delysia repeated. "What is the time?"

"Not yet ten o'clock, Miss."

Delysia sat up in bed.

"Well, I come from the country and I call that very late. Is no-one else awake?"

The maid pulled back the curtains and laughed.

"Her Ladyship's never called before noon and Miss Fleur'll often sleep 'til luncheon time."

There was obviously no chance of speaking to her sister this morning, and when the maid came back with her breakfast, she informed Delysia that Miss Fleur had said last night they would all be out for luncheon.

Delysia was up and dressed and waiting downstairs when finally Fleur appeared looking exquisitely lovely and not in the least tired after the exertions of the night before.

"Good morning, dearest," she said to Delysia. "You left the party far too early. It became very amusing later with some of the guests doing comic turns, but perhaps that would have shocked you."

"I enjoyed myself," Delysia replied, "but I was very tired and thought it would be embarrassing if I fell asleep!"

Fleur laughed.

"We merely would have thought you had had too much to drink!"

"I thought one or two of the Gentlemen were a trifle 'foxed'!" Delysia murmured.

She deliberately used the slang word that she had heard from her father, thinking it sounded less fault-finding.

Fleur laughed again.

"That is nothing new! The Earl, who I think is

rather a tiresome man, had to be carried downstairs by two of the footmen."

Delysia did not say anything, and then as if her sister was aware of what she was thinking she said sharply:

"Come on, we shall be late if we stay here talking."

"Where are we having luncheon?"

"Tim is taking us down to Ranelagh and we are going to watch Polo afterwards."

As she spoke the footman opened the door to say:

"His Lordship's here and he says will you hurry because his horses are fresh."

Delysia did not miss the eager way in which Fleur ran to the front door, with her eyes looking as if there was a light inside her.

Lord Sheldon was waiting for them in a very smart high-wheeled Phaeton, and it was fortunate they were both so slim for the vehicle was really only meant for two people.

Delysia, however, was feeling very touched because her sister was making such an effort to include her in everything she was doing.

As they drove to Ranelagh she was aware even more than she had been before, how very much in love Fleur was with Lord Sheldon and he with her.

Apart from what they said and the way they looked at each other, there were moments she knew when there was no need for words because they knew what each other was thinking.

The party was very much the same as it had been the night before, except that some of the men, but not Lord Sheldon, played Polo afterwards.

He and Fleur sat close together, talking to each

other in whispers and seemingly oblivious that a great number of other people present were watching them.

Delysia was however, uncomfortably aware that many of the glances they received were critical, and while she was glad to see her sister so happy there were obviously those who had a very different attitude.

By the time they returned to London, again in the Phaeton, she was growing more and more apprehensive, knowing there was something wrong.

As they reached the house and Lord Sheldon drew the horses up outside the front door, she heard Fleur ask:

"You will be dining with us tonight?"

"I hope so, my darling," Lord Sheldon replied, "but I do not know if my Uncle wants me."

"He has not—said anything?" Fleur asked in a hesitating tone.

Lord Sheldon shook his head.

"Not yet."

A footman helped Delysia down from the Phaeton to the ground, and when she looked back she saw Lord Sheldon kiss her sister's hand.

When Fleur joined her they went up the steps together, and to Delysia's relief the house seemed empty and there was no sign of Lady Matlock.

"I want to talk to you, Fleur."

"I expected that," her sister answered. "You had better come up to my bedroom. I must have a rest before I have to start changing for dinner."

Delysia followed her into the large impressive room which she remembered as being austere and rather masculine, as it had been used in the past by her father.

It certainly looked very feminine at the moment as there were great vases of flowers everywhere, a bedspread of lace over turquoise blue satin, and a profusion of soft satin cushions to relieve the dark upholstery of the chairs and sofa.

"Why did you choose this room?" Delysia asked.

"Beatrice wanted Mama's because it is so much prettier, and the Duke likes his women to be very feminine."

Delysia stiffened but felt it was a mistake to say anything, and Fleur, not realising that she had shocked her sister, continued:

"As it happens I have already ordered new curtains for this room, of peach velvet which will transform it, especially with an Aubusson carpet which I saw in Bond Street last week."

"Fleur, who is paying for all this?" Delysia asked.

"It is a mistake for you to ask questions."

"Dearest, I have to. You know quite well Papa will not pay the enormous bills you must be running up entertaining in such a lavish manner, and redecorating the rooms we danced in last night."

"Just leave it to me, Delysia, and do not fuss."

Delysia sat down in one of the chairs which was filled with pretty silk cushions.

"We never used to have any secrets," she said after a moment.

"That is true," Fleur agreed.

She turned round from the mirror in which she had been staring at her reflection and said in a different tone of voice:

"Oh, Delysia, I am so desperately unhappy!"

"Unhappy?" Delysia asked. "Why, dearest? I thought . . . in fact I was sure that you were in love."

"I am," Fleur said. "I love Tim madly and he loves me."

"Well, what is wrong?" Delysia asked. "I was thinking last night that you could be married at the end of the Summer when the garden will look beautiful, or perhaps you would want to be married in London."

"I would not care where I was married as long as I could marry Tim."

Fleur took off her bonnet and sat down on a low stool in front of the fireplace and put her hands over her eyes.

"Oh, Delysia—Delysia, what can I do?"

Delysia sprang out of the chair and there was just enough room for her on the stool beside her sister. She put her arms around her and as if she were a child held her close against her.

"Tell me what all this is about, darling," she said. "I am bewildered because I do not understand."

"I thought someone would have told you by now," Fleur said in a hard voice.

"Tell me what?"

"That Tim is engaged to be married."

"Engaged to be married?"

"Yes, it was announced two months ago before I met him."

"But dearest, in that case," Delysia began a little incoherently.

"Yes, I know, I know!" Fleur exclaimed. "We are behaving wildly and everyone is shocked! But we love each other, and I love him as Mama loved Papa! And from the moment he saw me he said it was impossible for him to think of anyone else."

Delysia's arms tightened around her sister.

"What can you do?"

"That is what he keeps asking," Fleur said.

Delysia was aware without Fleur telling her, that for a man to be officially engaged was as binding as if he were married.

A woman might break off an engagement, but never the man—unless he was to break an unwritten code of honour that was upheld by the members of every decent Club and every Regiment.

"His mother forced him into it," Fleur said, "because she is a snob and thinks no-one in the world is good enough for her son."

"Who is he engaged to?" Delysia enquired.

"The Duke of Dorset's daughter and Tim, although he was not in love with her, thought until he met me, they would get along well together."

Fleur gave a little cry before she said:

"Oh why, why did I not meet him until it was too late!"

"Was he not in London?" Delysia enquired.

"No, he was hunting with the Duke's pack and actually his home is in the same County, so of course he had actually known Elizabeth since they were children."

Fleur was silent as if she was thinking it over and then said:

"I did not think the Dorsets would have thought Tim grand enough for their only daughter, were he not so rich and with expectations from his uncle."

"I heard you mention his uncle as I got out of the Phaeton," Delysia said.

"Tim is frightened of him," Fleur said, "and I am terrified that now he has come to London he will forbid him to see me again."

"Do you think that he knows that you care for each other?" Delysia asked.

She thought as she spoke that if they were really trying to keep it a secret they were behaving in a very indiscreet manner, but there was no point in saying so.

After a moment Fleur said:

"I think Tim's mother will tell him, in fact I have a suspicion that she sent for her brother, Magnus Fane, simply because she knows Tim will not listen to anything she has to say against me."

"Who is Magnus Fane?" Delysia asked, thinking it was a strange name.

"According to Tim," Fleur replied, "he is a fantastic character out of a fairy story—the Demon King or the Ogre, and everyone trembles when he appears."

Delysia gave a little laugh because she could not help it and Fleur said:

"I promise you Delysia, it is no laughing matter as far as we are concerned. Tim's mother just sits and weeps and says her son will spoil his life if the Duke of Dorset finds out that he has already been unfaithful to his daughter, and his uncle, I am sure, will be even more formidable."

"What can he do?" Delysia asked curiously.

Fleur shrugged her shoulders.

"I do not know. Perhaps we are frightening ourselves unnecessarily. Mr. Fane has made a huge fortune out in the Far East where they treat him as if he were a King or something, but Tim is quite certain he is coming back to make trouble."

"He sounds horrid," Delysia agreed, "but at the same time it is Lord Sheldon's duty to behave in an honourable manner."

"I know all that," Fleur said, "but I love him and I shall die if I cannot marry him."

"You must not talk like that," Delysia said.

"Tim says he would shoot himself rather than marry another woman, and I believe him."

"Well, I do not! Lord Sheldon should not say such things to you," Delysia said sharply. "I think it was very wrong of him once he was engaged to someone else, to make you love him."

"There was no question of his making me love him," Fleur said with a little catch in her voice. "I knew as soon as he walked into the room he was the man of my dreams, and he is the reason why I refused all the proposals from all the other men who said they were in love with me."

Because she sounded so unhappy, Delysia wondered frantically what they could do.

"It is no use, dearest, you will have to be brave and send Lord Sheldon away."

Fleur jumped from the stool on which they were sitting.

"I will not do that! Nothing will make me! I love him and if, as he fears, his horrible uncle forbids us to see each other, we will run away together."

"No, Fleur!"

Delysia's voice seemed to echo around the room.

"You are not to do anything so outrageous! Think of the scandal it would cause, and afterwards no-one in the Social World which you enjoy so much would speak to you again."

"They would speak to me if I was Lady Sheldon and very rich," Fleur said, "especially if we lived abroad first for a year or so."

"You are not even to think of anything so disgraceful!"

"Mama ran away with Papa."

"I know, but she was not officially engaged to the Prince. In fact, Mama often said there was every likelihood that his Royal relatives would have prevented his marrying a commoner. Anyway, she caused scandal."

"If anyone runs away that always happens," Fleur said, "and if Papa had been a Lord, an Earl or a Marquis, they would have been forgiven far quicker than they were."

Delysia thought this was very probably true, and in fact by the time she was born, no-one cared that her father and mother had run away.

But she knew it would be very different if Lord Sheldon was to jilt anyone so important as the Duke of Dorset's daughter.

"Dearest Fleur, I am more sorry for you than I can possibly say!" she said. "But please be sensible and do what is the right thing. Give Lord Sheldon up now before there is any more trouble and come back to the country with me, if only for a month or so."

She thought if they could stay apart from each other things might get better.

Later when she left Fleur after pleading with her for nearly an hour, her sister had promised that she would think over what she had suggested.

As Delysia walked from the room she looked back to see Fleur lying on her bed looking beautiful and unhappy and she felt her heart ache.

"I am sorry, dearest," she said softly.

"I love you," Fleur answered, "but oh, Delysia, I love him so desperately."

That was again very obvious that night at dinner.

Lady Matlock was out with friends and the only guests were Lord Sheldon and Hugo Ludgrove.

Delysia had not been particularly pleased at having to see him again, but when he arrived he apologised so humbly for his behaviour the previous evening that she was touched by his sincerity.

"There is no excuse," he said, "except that I was up at dawn to attend a duel."

"A duel?" Delysia exclaimed.

"I had to support a friend," he replied. "He was fighting for the honour of a fair Lady."

Delysia knew it would be indiscreet to ask for further details and Hugo Ludgrove said:

"Actually, she was fair but not as beautiful as you. Anytime you need someone to defend you, count on me!"

"I hope there will never be a duel where I am concerned!" Delysia exclaimed.

"I would not be sure of it," he replied. "In fact, I am prepared to fight to the death any man who tries to take you from me!"

Delysia looked at him in astonishment and found he was looking at her in a manner she could not misinterpret and she felt the colour rise in her cheeks.

"You are so ridiculously beautiful," Hugo Ludgrove said, "and I am sure you realise that I have fallen hopelessly in love with you."

"I realise . . . nothing of . . . the sort," Delysia replied, "and I am sure it is . . . untrue."

"It is true!" he insisted. "But I will not upset you by saying too much until you are ready to listen to me."

Delysia felt shy, but she thought by the end of the evening he was very much nicer than she had thought him to be previously.

Lord Sheldon and Fleur ignored them completely and talked in low voices, so utterly absorbed in one another that Delysia thought despairingly that nothing she could say or do would make any difference.

At the same time, she knew that they were behaving very irresponsibly and that Lord Sheldon was to blame.

He was young but he had been brought up as a Gentleman, and she was aware from all her father had ever said that the unwritten code of gentlemanly behaviour was strict and unbreakable, unless a man was prepared to be branded as an outsider and a bounder.

Yet in a way she could understand how Fleur's beauty could blind any man to his responsibilities, and as she was as much in love with Lord Sheldon as he with her, it made the situation very difficult.

'Perhaps I could talk to him,' she thought to herself and was then aware that Hugo Ludgrove was watching the expression in her eyes.

"It is no use," he said in a low voice, "you can do nothing about it."

They were sitting at the other end of the Drawing

Room, and knowing what they said could not be over-heard, Delysia replied:

"We have to try. Please help me. My sister must not be involved in this manner."

She looked at Hugo Ludgrove pleadingly as she said:

"You know exactly what will happen. Lord Sheldon will be forced to marry the girl to whom he is engaged and will be forgiven for anything he has done, while Fleur will have to take all the blame and all the abuse earned by their behaviour will be heaped on her head."

She gave a little groan as she said:

"She will no longer be invited to the best parties and she will be ostracized by the Dowagers. She will be hurt, very hurt, besides having no-one to look after and protect her."

"I know exactly what you are saying," Hugo Ludgrove replied. "I have already talked to Tim, who will not listen to me."

"You must try again," Delysia said. "Please try again."

"I will do it for your sake," he said. "In fact I will do anything to stop your being so worried, although quite frankly I do not think Tim will listen to me, and I very much doubt that Fleur will listen to you."

"We have got to make them see sense," Delysia said. "And the longer they go on behaving as they are, the worse it will be."

"I agree with you there, but I cannot help feeling that someone else will take a hand at any moment and that Tim will have to listen to him."

"Are you speaking of his uncle?"

"Of course. I expect Fleur has told you about him."

"Have you met him?"

Hugo Ludgrove shook his head.

"He only arrived back in England a few days ago, but everyone who has been to the Far East knows about him and says he is the most powerful man out there."

"It frightens me even to hear about him!" Delysia said.

Hugo Ludgrove gave a smile.

"I will not let him hurt you, but I cannot guarantee he will not vent his anger on your sister."

"I cannot think that he could do anything really to hurt her," Delysia said defiantly. "After all, he can hardly put her in prison because his nephew is in love with her, and I cannot believe even the Demon King, as Fleur calls him, could injure her physically."

"No, I suppose not," Hugo Ludgrove agreed, "but when one thinks of the East one remembers the poisons that they have there, and the way those who cause trouble are spirited away never to be seen again."

"Now you *are* frightening me!" Delysia cried. "But we are in England and those sort of things do not happen here."

"Let us hope not," Hugo Ludgrove said, "and perhaps our argument to Tim should be what he is doing will hurt Fleur."

"That is clever of you!" Delysia exclaimed. "I am sure that is something he would listen to, in fact, he must."

Hugo Ludgrove put out his hand.

"We will do something about it together, shall we?"

"I would be very, very grateful for your help."

"My life is at your service," he replied.

As she put her hand in his he raised it gallantly to his lips.

Chapter Three

DELYSIA REALISED that Hugo Ludgrove was flirting with her.

But she was so worried about Fleur that she found it difficult to attend to him or listen to what he was saying.

She could see the clock on the mantelpiece from where she was sitting, and when the hands reached eleven o'clock she said:

"I hope you will not think it rude, Mr. Ludgrove, but I am tired and the Doctor, who made me come to London instead of going to Cheltenham with my father, insisted that I should take things very easy and have as much rest as possible."

"I understand," Hugo Ludgrove replied, "and I have heard how devotedly you nursed your father after his accident."

Delysia realised that while they were talking Fleur and Lord Sheldon had gone out on to the balcony which overlooked the small garden at the back of the house.

She thought it would be a mistake to disturb them, even though it might be a wise thing to do, and she therefore said:

"Tell Fleur I have retired. I know she will understand."

"I am sure she will," Mr. Ludgrove said, "at the same time I shall miss you."

He walked across the Drawing Room to open the door and as the main bedrooms were on the same floor, Delysia held out her hand and said:

"Thank you for saying you will help me. I am in fact, very very worried."

"I know you are," Hugo Ludgrove replied, "and I would give everything I possess to make you look as happy as your sister."

Again he was speaking in a way which made her feel a little shy, but she simply smiled and walked quickly to her bedroom without looking back.

When she reached it she realised she was almost as exhausted as she had been last night.

She despised herself for being so weak but knew it was what the Doctor had expected, and she was sure in a few days she would be her old self and ready for anything.

She thought with a sudden throb of her heart, if that included preventing Fleur from running away with Lord Sheldon, it was going to be a very exhausting task.

The maid helped her undress and as soon as she

got into bed Delysia, although she had expected to lie awake worrying, fell asleep.

She slept dreamlessly for what seemed a very long time and was awoken by the sound of a door shutting.

She thought it would be Fleur and decided although it was late, it might be a good time to talk to her.

She had the feeling that Lord Sheldon had brought her some news tonight. Perhaps when he went to his own house after they returned from Ranelagh, his uncle had been waiting for him and the interview he had been dreading had taken place.

'I am sure Fleur will want to tell me about it,' she thought.

She lit the candle by her bed, then got up and put on a warm wrap she had brought with her from the country.

She had thought when she saw the very beautiful and elegant nightgowns, chemises and negligees that Fleur had, the sooner she bought some new night things for herself the better.

Her day clothes were plain but in good taste.

Although she had not been able to come to London during her father's illness there was a dressmaker in the nearest town who could make what she required if she explained, almost stitch for stitch, what she wanted.

Her evening wardrobe, however, consisted of only two gowns, that were smart enough to wear at Fleur's parties, and she knew that the first thing she must do was to ask her sister to take her to a good dressmaker.

She could certainly not spend the very large sums which Fleur had been able to do, on her clothes, but at the same time she needed far more expensive and elegant gowns than she would ever wear in the country.

'But I do not want my sister to be ashamed of me,' she thought with a little smile.

She gave a quick glance in the mirror, tidied her hair and then opened her door.

The corridor was in darkness except for two candles in silver sconces which were always left alight at night and which by the morning had guttered into extinction.

Almost opposite the Rose Room, where she was sleeping, was her mother's room, and she was just passing the door when she stopped still and stiffened.

There was no doubt that inside Lady Matlock was talking to someone in her soft, somewhat artificial tones, and when a deep voice answered her, Fleur knew exactly who was there.

It was what she might have expected, but at the same time she was very shocked.

"Fleur must leave here tomorrow," she said to herself. "I will not have her staying in the same house with someone who behaves in such an outrageous manner."

It would be easier, she thought, if Lady Matlock left, because after all, the house did belong to Fleur's father.

At the same time she was uncomfortably aware that either Lady Matlock or perhaps even the Duke was paying for at least some of the extravagant way they were living.

Therefore it would really be easier for Fleur to return to Cousin Sarah and then ask Lady Matlock to leave.

It all seemed rather complicated and as Delysia hurried past the Boudoir she thought she would tell Fleur exactly what she felt about the whole situation, and not allow her to make excuses for her friend.

Her father's room, being in the corner of the building was entered by a door from the passage which opened first into a very small hall.

On one side of it was a hanging-cupboard and on the other a narrow, gold console table fixed to the wall.

The door into the bedroom was directly opposite.

Delysia opened the outer door and moved into the small hall. She actually had her hand on the handle of the door opposite when she heard Lord Sheldon say:

"My darling, I adore you, and nobody will make me lose you."

For a moment she thought she must be dreaming.

Then as her hand fell to her side she knew with a horror which was almost a physical pain, that Fleur was behaving in the same outrageous manner as Lady Matlock.

For a moment it was impossible to breathe, let alone move.

Then afraid she might be heard, she turned and crept back the way she had come, shutting the outer door very softly behind her.

It was only when she had reached her own bedroom that she was able to breathe again, and she stood for a long time with her back to the door thinking she was in a nightmare.

How could Fleur, her sister, whom she loved and

had tried to protect ever since her mother died, have a man in her bedroom, even though she had given him her heart?

"There is no excuse for such behaviour," Delysia murmured to herself.

But she thought she must have been stupid not to have realised from the very beginning that Fleur and Lady Matlock had taken over the family house simply so that they could be with the men they loved.

Why were they both behaving in a manner which would shock and horrify everyone who was at all respectable who became aware of it?

"How can Fleur do...anything so...wrong, so wicked?" Delysia asked.

Almost as if she herself wanted to hide, she crept into bed and started to cry.

She felt as if Fleur's life was passing her eyes in a series of pictures.

Fleur as a little girl running in the Park to pick daffodils.

Fleur riding in front of her father on his saddle.

Fleur sitting on his knee so that she could put her arms around his neck to kiss him goodnight.

Fleur crying bitterly when their mother died and later saying frantically:

"What shall we do—without her, Delysia? I know—you will look after me but I want—Mama."

The terrible thing was, Delysia thought, that she had not been able to look after her.

Fleur had gone her own way in her determination to go to London, and was now behaving in a manner which would break her mother's heart if she knew of it.

"Oh, Fleur! Fleur!" Delysia cried aloud with the tears running down her cheeks. "How could you do anything so disgraceful?"

She had never thought for one instant that Fleur would behave except like the young, innocent girl she had thought her to be.

She had vaguely heard about the temptations of London and how Gentlemen chased pretty girls and seduced them.

Delysia, although she was over twenty, had no idea exactly what this entailed, but she had never thought that it would apply to ladies like herself and her sister.

Although gentlemen would fall in love with someone as beautiful as Fleur and might even attempt to kiss her, she had no idea that their affection could be anything more dangerous.

Now she felt as if she had suddenly stepped down into a hell she did not even know existed, and there was evil all around her which was terrifying.

'I must talk to Fleur very, very seriously,' she decided.

She was ashamed that she felt weak at the thought and would rather, if she followed her inclination, run back home for security.

"If only I could talk to someone," she said aloud.

There was no-one to whom she could turn—least of all her father—who would only be furiously angry and doubtless make himself ill again.

"I have to deal with this myself," Delysia told herself, but she knew her real fear was that Fleur would not listen to her.

She slept very little and the hours seemed to crawl by before the dawn came.

Then as she heard the first sound of wheels in the street outside, she knew that before she faced Fleur and accused her of behaving so badly, she must go to Church.

It was Sunday and she had intended to suggest to her sister that they went to the Morning Service as they had always done at home.

She remembered that the Grosvenor Chapel, where her mother had taken them when they were last in London, was quite near.

She was sure there would be an early Communion Service which she could attend and it would give her strength to face Fleur later.

She rose and dressed, putting on her best Sunday gown, but wearing with it a small, rather plain bonnet instead of the large, more fashionable one which she had bought especially to come to London.

She knew if she behaved correctly she should ask one of the maids to go with her or the Housekeeper.

But she thought they might not be awake.

They would also have so much to do in the house that they would resent being taken away from their duties.

'I shall be quite all right on my own,' she thought. 'Grosvenor Chapel is only a few streets away and I shall be home before it is time for breakfast.'

She picked up her handbag and her prayer book which had been her mother's, and carrying them as well as her gloves, opened the door into the corridor.

She supposed by this time, although she was very vague about these things, that both the Duke and Lord Sheldon would have gone home.

As she did not want to think about them she hurried towards the top of the stairs and went down them quickly, noticing as she did so that the front door was open.

This meant that servants were stirring and she expected to see a mob-capped maid cleaning the front doorsteps.

There was, however, no-one there, nor was there a footman in attendance.

As she reached the front door she was just about to go out into the pale morning sunshine when she saw to her astonishment a large trunk.

It was one of her sister's which she recognised immediately. She had in fact, helped to pack it when Fleur had left home to come to London.

It was strapped up and as Delysia stood looking at it a frightening thought came into her mind.

Then suddenly a man's voice behind her asked:

"Are you Miss Langford?"

She turned her head and saw a man who was obviously a servant, and behind him, without her being aware of it, a closed carriage drawn by two horses had just come to a standstill at the bottom of the steps.

"Yes, I am Miss Langford," she replied.

Then she gave a frightened scream.

As she spoke, the man had thrown a thick black cloth over the top of her and before she could even realise what was happening, he picked her up in his arms.

A moment later she found herself placed none too

carefully on what she was aware was the back seat of a carriage.

Then as the carriage door was shut, there was the sound of something heavy being dumped overhead and the horses drove off.

Delysia was not only astonished at what had happened, but she also felt as if the breath had been knocked out of her body.

She only began to struggle when she felt hands at her ankles and was aware that the man was tying something round them.

It was not a rope but a piece of material which did not hurt but made it impossible for her to move.

She tried to push away the cloth which covered her, as she thought, from her head to below her knees, but before she could move her arms something else restricting, a strap or a scarf, was tied round her waist.

It struck her she was trussed up like a hen and completely immobile.

The man did not speak but she was aware he was sitting opposite her on the small seat of the carriage and because she was frightened she did not try to use her voice.

What was painful was that the heavy cloth had pushed her bonnet down her forehead so that she could feel the crushed straw digging into her skin.

'What can this mean? Who can have kidnapped me?' she wondered.

Suddenly she knew what had occurred, and though it seemed incredible, more like something out of a story book, she was sure it was true.

The man who had come to the door from the carriage thought she was Fleur.

When she had agreed she was Miss Langford and he had seen the trunk beside her, he did not question that she was the person he was seeking.

There was no need to ask who wished to kidnap Fleur or who was the only person who could have known or guessed what she was doing.

It was very hard to breathe beneath the thick cloth that covered her, but Delysia's brain seemed to be racing in her head as she thought out the whole fantastic chain of events and was sure she had the clue to the puzzle.

Fleur and Lord Sheldon had intended to run away together this morning as her sister had threatened to do.

Perhaps they had been impelled to do so immediately by something which Magnus Fane had said last night to his nephew before he came to dinner.

Whatever it was, they had obviously arranged to leave early this morning before anyone was awake.

The night footman would have brought down Fleur's trunk and he had perhaps gone back for another, which was why he was not on the door.

Magnus Fane, and she knew now that he really was a Demon King, had guessed or had been told by some informant what was going to occur, and he had therefore determined to spirit Fleur away before his nephew could reach her.

Unfortunately, because she—Delysia, had wished to go to Church they had the wrong sister.

It seemed incredible, but thinking it out very carefully, Delysia was sure that was what happened.

'Wherever he is taking me,' Delysia thought, 'Mr. Fane will have a distinct shock when I tell him who I am!'

Because she had conceived a dislike of him ever since Fleur had spoken about him, though she really had no reason to do so, she felt it would be a satisfaction to see him discomfitted.

'He had no right to do anything so outrageous as to kidnap my sister,' she thought. 'He should have been gentleman enough to discuss the situation with her and persuade her, as I intended to do, to sacrifice herself for the man she loved.'

Delysia nevertheless had the uncomfortable feeling that her pleading would not have been effective, and she was certain Fleur would not have listened to Magnus Fane.

At the same time it would have been the correct way to do things, rather than to think up anything so terrible as to kidnap a young girl.

Then as they drove on, the horses moving very swiftly, so that Delysia was sure that they were well bred and well trained, she suddenly realised that Magnus Fane, by his outrageous action had in fact, made it easy for Fleur and Lord Sheldon to elope without any interference.

They might find one trunk was missing, but that would not deter them.

In fact, Delysia knew that the amount of clothes Fleur had bought since she had come to London would fill half a dozen trunks.

She wondered how she could persuade Magnus Fane as soon as she met him that they must go back immediately to try to prevent Lord Sheldon taking Fleur out of the country.

She was certain this was what Lord Sheldon would do and that they would go to Paris, since it was easier to get to France than anywhere else.

Or perhaps they would choose Italy. She remembered Fleur had always wanted to see Rome.

The horses travelled on, and Delysia began to feel extremely uncomfortable with her arms clamped to her side and unable to move her feet.

She realised that the blanket over her was so thick that it would be difficult to make herself heard if she spoke and, what was more, shouting through a thick cloth would make her even more undignified than she was already.

She felt her anger rising because she was so helpless and because the whole thing had become a hopeless muddle.

While Magnus Fane was having her conveyed to some unknown destination, Fleur and Lord Sheldon were running away without anyone to stop them or try to persuade them to see sense.

"This is ridiculous! Absolutely ridiculous!" Delysia said.

Because she was angry she no longer felt frightened.

Magnus Fane would certainly not injure her in fact the only thing he could do would be to apologise profusely for the way she had been treated.

He would then post after his nephew and Fleur, although it was doubtful if he would be able to find them.

'Perhaps his spies told him where they are going,' Delysia thought contemptuously.

She had always disliked people who used their servants and perhaps even their friends to extract information which otherwise they would not have known.

Yet she supposed those who lived in the East thought it a quite usual way of behaviour, and perhaps she should be thankful Magnus Fane had not poisoned her as Hugo Ludgrove had suggested he might.

'Fleur should never have got mixed up in all this,' she thought.

Once again she was blaming herself for not having found out sooner that Fleur had left Lady Barlow and become involved with someone like Lady Matlock.

She was still extremely shocked, as she had been last night, when she had been aware that the Duke was in Lady Matlock's bedroom and Fleur was behaving in the same manner.

She wanted to find excuses for her, even though she knew it was so disgraceful that she had no wish to think about it.

The carriage travelled on and on, and Delysia began to wonder where she was being taken.

She suspected if he was Lord Sheldon's uncle and Where did he live when he was in England, and how old was he?

She suspected if he was Lord Sheldon's uncle and was as rich and important as he was reputed to be, he would be perhaps over fifty.

Whatever his age she was sure he was a dictator and a tyrant to all those who were associated with him.

'I expect he told his nephew he was to give up seeing Fleur without giving him a chance to explain what he felt for her, and this drove them to act so precipitately,' she thought.

More miles seemed to have passed before she said to herself:

"It is his fault, all his fault, and I shall tell him so."

They must have been driving nearly two hours before Delysia felt with an overwhelming relief, the horses were drawing slowly to a standstill.

She was sure they had been in the open country for a long time, but they had slowed down only occasionally to pass other traffic and there had been no stops of any sort.

Now at last, they must have arrived and she wondered whether it would be at a country house and, if it was, what she would say to Magnus Fane as soon as she met him.

She realised because it was very hot and airless under the cloth, that her cheeks must be flushed and with her bonnet crushed down on her forehead, her hair untidy. So it would be hard to be dignified.

But by this time she did not care.

"I shall tell him exactly what I think of him and his outrageous behaviour!" she stormed. "Papa too, would think it a disgraceful act on the part of a Gentleman!"

Then the door of the carriage was opened and the man who had been sitting opposite her spoke to someone outside.

A moment later he picked her up off the seat and

carried her a short distance over soft ground. Then she heard his footsteps on a wooden floor.

It seemed rather strange and Delysia tried to imagine where she could possibly be going, when unexpectedly she was carried down some steep steps.

This was even more puzzling and she suddenly thought with a stab of fear that Magnus Fane might be meaning to imprison her in a crypt, or perhaps a cellar.

Then she was carried through what she was sure was a doorway, because the man who had his arms around her had to turn sideways.

She was put down on something soft. The moment he did so, he untied first the scarf from her legs and then loosened whatever had been tied round her waist.

She did not move and she thought perhaps he would now lift the blanket off her face. Instead she heard his footsteps receding.

A door shut, and as she held her breath she was certain she was alone.

Still Delysia waited and tried to sense if there was anyone watching her in the room.

She was extremely reluctant to face in such an ignominious position her captor, who she was sure was Magnus Fane.

Now very angry, she listened in case she could hear someone breathing.

Suddenly she heard footsteps ringing overhead and voices shouting to each other, and a moment later, the bed or whatever she was lying on, began to move and Delysia knew she was in a ship.

She sat up abruptly and pushed back the blanket

that had covered her.

Her first glance told her that she was right, she was in a cabin on a ship which was now moving, she supposed, out of some harbour.

As the blanket, and it was a very thick one, fell back on the bed behind her she struggled to her feet and went to the porthole.

The one in her cabin was, she was surprised to notice, elegantly framed with green velvet curtains, but at the moment all that concerned her was to look outside.

She saw as she expected that they were moving away from a quay, passing a number of other ships, and the bar of the harbour was just ahead with the open sea beyond.

Delysia gave a gasp.

It could not be true! How could it be possible that she had been kidnapped and was being conveyed not only from her father's house but actually out of England?

Then as the wind caught the sails, the ship veered to starboard and she hastily put out her hands to steady herself, then sat down on a chair that was battened to the floor.

She realised as she did so that in front of her was a mirror and she looked in it with horror.

Her straw bonnet was crushed, bent and pressed down on her head which made her, she thought, look grotesque.

She quickly pulled it off and threw it onto the floor, knowing she could never wear it again.

Then she wiped her face with her handkerchief,

feeling that it was not only damp having been confined beneath the blanket, but also dirty from the contact with it.

She had no comb, but she tidied her hair as best she could.

Then as she looked round she realised that Fleur's trunk that she knew had been carried on top of the carriage was just inside the door.

Someone must have put it there while her abductor was loosening her legs and removing the sash which had been put round her waist.

Delysia looked at the trunk and decided that if Magnus Fane had taken the trouble to order that Fleur's luggage should come with her, he certainly intended to keep her a prisoner for some time.

It puzzled Delysia to think where the ship could be going, and she wondered whether she should hammer on the door to attract attention and demand to see Magnus Fane immediately before they were too far out to sea.

'Every moment we are sailing further and further away in this absurd fashion,' she thought, 'Fleur and Lord Sheldon will be driving to Dover.'

She had an idea, though she could not be sure, that the nearest harbour to London would be somewhere in the Thames Estuary and that could be reached in about the time the horses had taken to bring her to the ship.

"I must see Mr. Fane at once," she told herself.

But she could not help shrinking at what she was sure was going to be a very unpleasant interview.

She was still wondering whether it would be best to wait until Magnus Fane sent for her or demand to see him, when there was the sound outside the cabin.

She sat up very straight but she could not prevent herself from being frightened, and watching the door as it opened.

A man came in who was obviously a steward, carrying expertly despite the moving ship, a tray.

"I've brought you some breakfast, Miss," he said cheerily. "I thought you'd best eat it as soon as possible as there's a spot of wind and the sea may be rough later."

He put the tray down in front of her on what she realised was a dressing table and said:

"If there's anything else you'd like, Miss, I'll get it for you."

Not waiting for a reply, and while Delysia was wondering what to say, he left the cabin.

As she looked at the tray, because she had had very little to eat last night, she was glad to see there was a pot of coffee.

She poured herself out a cup, then as she thought they would give her the courage she vitally needed, she ate the eggs which were well-cooked and the hot toast which she spread with butter and honey.

'I have to be very firm,' she decided.

She however, knew that, because of her exhausted state, food was essential if she was not to be very limp or even faint after what she had been through.

She certainly felt better after eating and drinking two cups of coffee.

She was aware the ship was moving very swiftly and she was sure that the wind filling the sails was behind them.

It was not really rough, only uncomfortable, when

they changed course, but she was sure if she had been on deck it would have been exhilarating to move at such a speed.

Delysia had been yachting with her father along the South Coast in the summer some years ago and it was a relief to know she was a good sailor.

At the same time, she was not concerned with herself but with Fleur, and she waited until the steward returned, then said:

"Would you be so kind as to inform me what this ship is and to whom it belongs?"

He grinned at her.

"I thought you knew, Miss. It's Mr. Magnus Fane who's the owner and *The Sea Lion* is the new yacht he ordered afore he went East and only came from the shipbuilders a month ago."

There was a note of pride in his voice as he added:

"Built along the same lines as the American clippers, and there ain't anything around these shores as'd beat it in a race."

Delysia drew in her breath.

"Is Mr. Magnus Fane on board?"

"Of course, Miss."

"Would you be kind enough to inform him I would like to speak to him as soon as possible."

"I will tell him, Miss. But he's been watching the ship leave harbour and won't want to be disturbed."

"Will you please inform him it is urgent?"

Delysia thought the steward smiled in a somewhat impertinent manner as if he knew that would not impress Mr. Fane, but he picked up the tray and walked from the cabin saying:

"I'll tell him, Miss."

'Mr. Fane is going to look very stupid,' Delysia thought to herself as she waited. 'He has taken all this trouble to spirit Fleur away from his nephew and has taken the wrong person.'

She felt her anger rising again with what she considered his disgraceful behaviour, yet when the steward returned to say that Mr. Fane would see her in the Saloon, she felt not angry but afraid.

Now she was going to confront the Demon King, or perhaps he was better described as the Ogre who was also a kidnapper.

It was difficult walking on a slant to be as dignified as she wished, but somehow she managed it.

A steward opened a door and she walked in to what was one of the prettiest ship's Saloons she had ever seen.

Then as the man who was waiting for her at the end of it rose to his feet, she saw he was not in the least what she had expected.

Chapter Four

IT HAD BEEN so firmly established in Delysia's mind that Magnus Fane was an elderly man that she was astonished to see that although he was not very young, he was certainly not old.

He was tall, extremely good-looking, with broad shoulders and very slim.

Although he was fashionably dressed, she had the quick impression that his clothes were comfortable and that he was not concerned with them.

As she was staring at him, he was looking at her with an expression that she knew immediately was one of anger and contempt.

He did not speak and she walked steadily, although it was difficult with the movement of the ship, towards him.

When they were only a few feet apart, Delysia

deliberately dropped him a small curtsy and then stood waiting.

She had, however, to reach out to hold on to the back of a chair and he said abruptly:

"Sit down!"

She obeyed him, moving as slowly as she could to show her independence.

The chair was comfortable and as she sat on the edge of it and put her hands in her lap, she looked down, thinking that in a few moments Magnus Fane would be apologising to her for mistaking her for Fleur.

At the same time she could feel her heart beating in a violent manner and knew despite the fact that her mind told her she was in the right, she was frightened.

"I imagine, Miss Langford," Magnus Fane began in a sharp voice, "that you are surprised at finding yourself on board my yacht, but I am determined to prevent you from ruining my nephew's life."

He paused as if he expected Delysia to speak, but she deliberately kept quiet and he went on:

"When I learnt very early this morning that you had inveigled him into running away with you, I was appalled, and only by swift action have I prevented you both from doing anything so outrageous!"

He spoke in a hard, aggressive voice which made Delysia sure that was how he habitually spoke to his inferiors.

She knew she had been right when she thought of him as a dictator and a tyrant, and she felt her hatred for him rising inside her.

Magnus Fane continued:

"I have learnt since I returned from the East of the

way you and my nephew have been living together in your father's house. I imagine Sir Kendrick is not aware of your behaviour, and if there are any results from such immoral behaviour, I wish to inform you here and now that I will not allow my nephew to be held responsible."

For a moment Delysia did not understand what he meant.

Then as if forked lightning had struck her she suddenly understood., He was insinuating, although it seemed incredible that he should do so, that Fleur might have a baby!

Such an idea had never entered her mind, but now that the full impact of what Magnus Fane was saying was clear, she thought she would faint at the horror of it.

She gripped her hands together in her lap until her knuckles showed white.

Then as she wanted to protest and say it was something that could never happen, she knew that the only thing that mattered was that Fleur should be married to Lord Sheldon.

Suddenly, as if it was a light shining in the darkness in which she had been plunged, she knew that the only piece of good fortune was that she was here and not Fleur.

At this very moment, while Magnus Fane was accusing her of something which she still could not believe Fleur had done, she and Lord Sheldon would be on their way abroad.

If they were not married before they left England, they would be as soon as they set foot on foreign soil.

As it all flashed through Delysia's mind, she realised that the situation was now completely reversed and whatever happened, Fleur must now not be prevented from becoming a married woman.

She still found it hard to credit that her sister whom she loved and always wanted to protect, should have done anything so incredibly wrong as to allow a man to make love to her without being married.

What was more, that she had not foreseen what might be the consequences of such a foolhardy action.

But because Fleur loved Tim Sheldon and he loved her, and because she knew they had been together last night, Delysia could only pray fervently that her sister might not be stigmatised for all time by having an illegitimate child.

She had never in her wildest forebodings imagined anything so terrible, but she knew now that the real disaster would be for Magnus Fane to interfere and force them apart.

"They must be married, of course they must be married!" Delysia said in her heart.

She knew the only way to make sure of this was for her to pretend to be her sister until such time as their wedding was announced. Then there would be nothing Magnus Fane could do about it.

She knew she was trembling from the shock of what she had just realised. Yet even while her nails dug into her skin she forced herself to remain seated stiffly upright, her eyes cast down.

"You will therefore understand," Magnus Fane said, "that I intend to keep you out of the way until my nephew comes to his senses and marries the girl to whom he is engaged."

As he finished speaking Delysia, without looking

at him, was aware he was looking at her speculatively as if he were surprised by her silence.

Because she thought that she must in some way defend Fleur against the condemnation in his voice, she said quietly:

"I presume, Mr. Fane, you are not concerned with your nephew's happiness?"

"Happiness?" Magnus Fane exclaimed. "I suppose by that you mean that because he is young and foolish he thinks he would find happiness with you!"

Again he paused, expecting Delysia to reply, but as she did not, he went on:

"I have made it my business, Miss Langford, to enquire into your past. It is not a very long one, but it is highly coloured with incidents which convey nothing to your credit!"

Delysia lifted up her chin.

"I do not know why you should say that, Mr. Fane."

"Do you want chapter and verse?" he asked sarcastically. "Very well. I have heard how you pursued the Marquess of Gazebrooke, until he very wisely left London for the country. How you enveigled various other young peers to dance attendance on you until either their families or their own good sense prevented them from making the offer of marriage you were seeking."

He made a derisive sound before he continued:

"I can assure you, your reputation is very lurid for someone so young, and after this last escapade I imagine that most of the doors in Mayfair will be closed to you!"

He spoke with a satisfaction in his voice which made Delysia more angry than she was already.

However she knew it was no use claiming that the Marquess had proposed marriage, but Fleur had refused him.

Although she believed her sister, she was quite certain Magnus Fane would not do so, and she had frankly to admit that there might be just a grain of truth in the accusations he had thrown at her.

She felt, however, that she must make one more effort on Fleur's behalf.

"I suppose, Mr. Fane, you would not believe me if I told you that I love your nephew with all my heart, just as he loves me."

"Real love, Miss Langford," Magnus Fane replied, "is something which I cannot believe is within your comprehension or that you would understand anything about it!"

"That is where you are wrong," Delysia answered, "and since you are condemning me on hearsay, it is only fair that I should ask you if you yourself know anything about love."

She saw the surprise as she spoke, in Magnus Fane's eyes, and he raised his eyebrows as if he thought she was being impertinent before he said:

"We were talking about you, Miss Langford, and I cannot imagine that you would marry my nephew if he were not rich, titled, and what I believe is popularly called a 'good catch.'"

"I assure you that is completely untrue," Delysia said positively. "I would marry him if he had not a penny to his name and if we had to live in a mud hut and beg for our food."

She spoke with a ring of sincerity in her voice because she was speaking for Fleur.

She knew that what her sister felt for Tim Sheldon was the same love that her mother had for her father when they had run away together.

For a moment Magnus Fane looked surprised, then he said:

"Pretty words, but easy to say when the situation has not arisen."

He was sneering at her and Delysia said:

"Love is something which cannot be bought and it eludes a great many people to their sorrow. But when one has once found real love, it is irresistible and no-one is strong enough to refuse it!"

She thought as she spoke that he looked more cynical than ever and she added angrily:

"What you are doing is condemning two people who genuinely love each other, to a life of misery and loneliness. Worst of all, because you are blinded by social convention you are forcing your nephew into a marriage which can only be disastrous."

"If you want the truth," Magnus Fane said, "I can imagine nothing more disastrous for him than to be married to you."

His manner was so rude that Delysia could hardly believe any Gentleman could speak in such a way.

She rose to her feet and holding onto the back of the chair to support herself, she said;

"I cannot expect, Mr. Fane, after all I have heard of you, that you should be anything but prejudiced and thus constitute yourself in this instance both judge and jury. All I can say is that it is very unfair and certainly very unsporting!"

She then turned round and walked as quickly as she could in order to keep her balance out of the Saloon and down the companionway to her cabin.

Inside it, she sat down on the bed and then because she could not help it, she began to cry.

"How could anyone be so horrible and so vindictive to Fleur?" she asked.

Although she was terribly shocked and upset by her sister's behaviour, she knew that the reason for it was quite simple: Fleur was in love—overwhelmingly and completely in love.

She began to pray with a note of desperation in her voice:

"Please, God, do not let him be successful in separating them. Fleur must marry Tim! Once they are married and happy together, nothing else will matter."

At the same time, she was terribly afraid that, even when they were married, Magnus Fane would be so bitterly antagonistic to Fleur that he would find some way of separating her from her husband.

Then she told herself she was being needlessly apprehensive about that. If the marriage was legal, then there would be nothing he could do.

She thought that perhaps there might be some grounds for saying the marriage could not be valid since Fleur was under age and her guardian had to give his consent.

But Delysia was sure that her father, who adored Fleur, would not only refuse to interfere with any marriage she made, but would actually be sympathetic because he himself had run away with their mother.

"It will be all right," she whispered reassuringly, "if they have time to get married and stay abroad for a short while where Magnus Fane cannot find them."

She was certain that Tim Sheldon would want to

do this anyway, so as to avoid any recriminations from the Duke of Dorset and his daughter. It was all very complicated and frightening.

At the same time it was quite clear to Delysia that she had to play the part of her sister until Fleur was safe.

She felt her heart sink at the thought, knowing that Magnus Fane was the most intimidating person she had ever known.

She found herself remembering how Hugo Ludgrove had said he would fight for her and she only had to call upon him to do so.

That would certainly not be very easy, when he had no idea where to find her and she did not even know where she was being taken.

She had the feeling that wherever it was, it would be unpleasant.

She wondered how she would be able to endure for long being in the company of Magnus Fane and undoubtedly hearing him abuse her for sins that Fleur might or might not have committed.

One thing of which she was quite certain was that Fleur had no need to run after men, as Magnus Fane had insinuated.

They had run after her ever since she was little more than a child, and Delysia was quite certain that Fleur had been truthful when she had said that the men whom she had found unattractive had all proposed marriage.

Delysia had always been able to tell when her sister was trying to deceive her, and in fact, because their mother and father had both disliked lies they invariably from the time they were very small, told the truth.

75

"Magnus Fane has never seen Fleur, so he has no idea how lovely she is," Delysia reasoned. "The best thing I can do is to be charming and good-mannered however rude he may be. Perhaps through me he will get a different idea of what Fleur is really like."

She told herself this was a sensible plan of action for the simple reason that, whether he liked it or not, Fleur was going to be married to his nephew, and inevitably they would encounter each other a great deal in the future.

She also knew that although Tim Sheldon was already a wealthy man having inherited his father's estate, he hoped in addition to benefit from his uncle who was enormously rich.

It was then that Delysia remembered that Magnus Fane was not likely to die for a very long time.

She was still astonished to have seen that he was comparatively young, when she had expected an ageing, grey-haired old man.

Indeed from his looks she reckoned that although he was certainly over thirty, he could not be more than thirty-five at the most.

"I suppose he must be brilliant to have won such a position at such an early age," she admitted. "But things are different in the East. An Englishman can have powers out there which he would not have in England."

She supposed it was silly of her not to have asked Fleur but it was clear that Tim Sheldon's mother must be the sister of Magnus Fane, but a great deal older than he was.

"I should have asked more questions," Delysia told herself.

Yet who could have dreamt that she would find herself in the position she was in, and known that Fleur's whole happiness depended on her playing a part cleverly.

"I was never a good actress, even in the charades we acted at home," Delysia told herself despairingly.

But because she loved her sister she knew that she had to make sure that Fleur was safely married before she revealed her identity.

What was the use of having always believed that she was intelligent, if she could not deceive Magnus Fane?

She had the uncomfortable idea that he would be perceptive, simply because no man could be as successful as he had been unless he had that rare sixth sense which was essential in dealing with human beings, whatever their creed or colour.

'Whatever happens, he must not use it on me,' Delysia resolved.

She told herself again that she must be charming.

If she could reverse the erroneous impression he had formed of Fleur, which could only have originated from women who had disliked or envied her, then things might be even better in the future, than Tim Sheldon hoped.

Once again she prayed that Fleur and Tim would be married as quickly as possible without anyone preventing them from doing so.

Then it occurred to her that if she had to stay with Magnus Fane she would need clothes, and realised it was a good thing that her kidnappers had been thoughtful enough to bring one of Fleur's trunks with her.

She opened it and found that, although it was filled mostly with attractive gowns, there was also what she most needed at the moment—a warm coat!

It was one that she had never seen before, and was obviously intended to be worn on smart occasions.

Although it was made of satin and elegantly braided, it was also bordered with fur.

It was obviously a very expensive fur, and Delysia did not like to guess what it had cost.

However, since it was the only coat in the trunk, she knew that unless she was to sit in her cabin the whole of the voyage she would have to wear it.

It did not look right with her own gown which she had put on to go to Church, so she looked and found a frock which she was certain had been designed to wear under the coat.

Fortunately she and Fleur were about the same size, but she laughed at her appearance in the mirror thinking that she looked far too elegant to be a prisoner of Magnus Fane on the way to some kind of penitentiary.

Because her only bonnet had been battered beyond repair, she found a long length of blue chiffon which she put over her head and wound the end round her neck to keep it in place.

It framed her small pointed face which was now dominated by eyes that were too large for it, because she had become so thin and run down through looking after her father.

It did in fact, make her look quite lovely and somewhat ethereal, although Delysia did not think about herself in that way.

In her opinion at any rate, Fleur was so much the lovelier that there was no comparison between them.

When she was ready, Delysia determinedly walked out of her cabin, up the companionway and onto the deck.

She was experienced enough to decide to go to windward where the sunshine and the freshness of the air seemed to sweep away not only some of her fatigue after all she had been through but also her fear.

She found somewhere to sit and leant back with the sun on her face, thinking of how much she loved being at sea, and that she might as well enjoy this if nothing else.

She must have been on deck for over a quarter-of-an-hour before there came a shadow between her and the sun.

She looked up to see Magnus Fane looking at her in surprise.

He had changed from the clothes he had been wearing in which she thought he must have travelled, and he was now in a yachting jacket and wore a peaked cap on his head.

To her surprise he said, in a voice different from any he had used to her before:

"Are you quite comfortable, Miss Langford?"

Delysia smiled.

"What you are really asking is if I feel sea-sick. The answer is 'no.' I am a very good sailor. I love the sea."

Magnus Fane sat down beside her.

"That surprises me," he said. "I thought most women were sea-sick at the first wave and lay in the cabins moaning until they reached dry land."

"I have sailed with my father in some very rough weather," Delysia replied, "and I must congratulate you, Mr. Fane, on your new yacht. I can see it is very attractive, and I have never travelled so fast on water, as we are doing now."

She thought as she spoke, with a little inward smile of amusement, that they were talking like two people who had just been introduced to each other at a Social Regatta, rather than captor and captive.

"I am very pleased with the yacht myself," Magnus Fane replied, "and if you are interested I would like to show you round it. I have introduced many innovations that are new to the English ship-builders."

"I would very much like to see it," Delysia replied, "and I think *The Sea Lion* is a very appropriate name."

When they sat down to luncheon she had an impulse to giggle at the way she and Magnus Fane were behaving.

She had the feeling that he had reasoned as she had, that it would be absurd to go on fighting if they were to be together for any length of time.

He spoke to her as he would have to any lady guest and she made herself as pleasant as she could, not forgetting to praise everything he showed her.

She was, however, careful not to look at him directly more often than was necessary.

She was quite sure that if she did so he would see that she disliked him, and she was terribly afraid he might penetrate her pretence.

She thought that if he did have the sixth sense of which she was afraid, it would be easier for him to read her thoughts by looking at her eyes than by listening to what she said.

"One can disguise one's tone of voice and make it at least impersonal," she reasoned. "But I am sure, although I have never thought of it before, it is difficult to control the truth from shining from the depths of one's eyes."

During luncheon she persuaded Magnus Fane to talk about the East.

"I think Tim told me you were in India," she said.

"That is where I started long before I was my nephew's present age," Magnus Fane answered. "I was first with the East India Company, then on my own."

"How did you become so rich and powerful?"

"I admit the first, but not necessarily the second," he replied with a smile.

"That is being ultra-modest," Delysia said. "Everyone has frightened me by telling me how overwhelmingly powerful you are."

"Are you frightened of me?" Magnus Fane asked unexpectedly. "You are not showing any signs of it."

"What do you want me to do?" Delysia asked. "Kneel at your feet and beg for mercy?"

She spoke teasingly as she might have spoken to Fleur and saw the surprise in his eyes.

Then because she was anxious not to offend him she said quickly:

"I will behave like a penitent, if that is what you wish me to do, but I am sure that after the first moments of satisfaction you would find it very boring."

As if he could not help himself, Magnus Fane laughed.

"You are certainly unpredictable, Miss Langford!"

"That is a relief and a compliment," Delysia replied, "for I find nothing more boring than knowing exactly what people are going to say and do, and I am sure you do too."

Before he could speak she gave a little sigh and said:

"You are so lucky, so very, very lucky! You have travelled all over the world, as I should love to do. You have met people of every nation, and while you have lived among them, I have merely read about them."

Again Magnus Fane looked surprised.

"My reports on you, Miss Langford, did not include the information that you are a reader."

"Now you know that I am. I very much hope you have a few books on board."

"I have, as it happens, in my own cabin," Magnus Fane replied, "but I doubt they are what you would find enjoyable."

"Once again you are going on hearsay, instead of your own observation," Delysia said without thinking.

As she spoke she thought she had made a mistake, for what she had said would perhaps make him more perceptive about her than he would have been otherwise.

But he laughed and answered:

"I can certainly test you, and if you are interested in India, I have quite a number of books about that mysterious and, to me, very exciting country."

Because she asked him intelligent questions she found the luncheon far more enjoyable than she had expected, and she had the feeling that he did too.

When they finished what had been an excellently cooked meal served by two stewards, Magnus Fane said:

"I shall be delighted to show you my Library, but where we are going there is a far larger one, although

I suspect the books are somewhat out of date."

"You have not yet told me what our destination is," Delysia replied. "I was rather afraid it might be Devil's Island, or some other convict settlement from which there is no escape."

"There *will* be no escape!" Magnus Fane averred firmly. "But I do not think you would describe it as Devil's Island."

He rose from the table as he spoke and they went down the companionway and past Delysia's cabin to the stern of the ship.

Here she found what she knew was the Master Suite, which was, as might have been expected, quite palatial.

It was a large cabin which contained the traditional Captain's four-poster and was hung with beautifully woven crimson velvet curtains, and she felt that somehow this combination of luxury with good taste was characteristic of him.

Beside it was a Sitting-Cabin which was certainly very different from any Delysia had ever seen before.

There were two obviously valuable pictures of ships by great masters, and one wall was entirely covered with books.

The sofa and chairs, which were of course battened down onto the floor on which was a thick carpet, were upholstered in red leather which matched the curtains over the portholes.

As if she had asked the question, Magnus Fane explained:

"I have grown used to brilliant colours and miss them when they are not there."

"I can understand that," Delysia said. "I have always believed that colour stimulates the mind and can give us spiritual energy."

She spoke without thinking and did not see the surprise in Magnus Fane's eyes as she moved instinctively towards the bookcase.

There were a large number of books, and as she looked at them Delysia was certain she would like the time to read every one of them.

There were books on India and other parts of the East.

There were also books on Philosophy which she was certain she would enjoy, and quite a number, which she had not expected, of poetry.

Again as if he knew what she was thinking, Magnus Fane said:

"If you are comparing the love we spoke of earlier in the day with that expressed by the poets, I can only say you are mistaken."

"Why?"

"Because the poets are writing of an idealistic love which some of us seek but never find. It is an emotion which is not to be found in Ball-Rooms, or among those who care for nothing but money and position."

Again he was speaking in that scathing, aggressive tone in which he had addressed her when she had first come aboard.

She did not answer, instead she merely drew a book from the shelves and opened it.

It was *The Lay of the Last Minstrel* by Sir Walter Scott, and she turned over a few pages before she found what she sought.

Then she read very quietly:

Love rules the Court, the Camp, the grove
And men below and Saints above
For Love is Heaven and Heaven is Love.

There was no answer from Magnus Fane.

He walked away from her to stand at a porthole looking out to sea.

Delysia did not turn round. She merely closed the book and put it under her arm.

Then she took from another shelf one on India.

"May I read these?" she asked. "I promise I will take great care of them."

"Yes, of course," he replied.

He did not look at her, and she had the feeling he was thinking of something else.

She glanced at him tentatively for a moment. Then she said:

"I expect you want to be on the bridge steering the ship. Shall I go to my cabin so as to be out of your way?"

"I expect you would rather be on deck."

"I would like that, if I would not be any trouble."

She thought, although she was not certain, that he was rather surprised at her reply, but as he had obviously agreed she should do what she wished, she left the cabin to go to her own.

As she put the books down on her bed she told herself with a little smile she had at least made him begin to think about Fleur in a new way.

She was sure he had expected either an exhibition of temper, or else tears, sulks, and frenzied pleadings to be taken home.

"What I have to do," Delysia told herself, "is to make sure that when he finally learns I am not Fleur, he will have formed in his mind an entirely different picture of what she is like to what he thought about her before."

At the moment it seemed very difficult.

She had not forgotten the way Magnus Fane had denounced her as soon as they met, and she was certain he was not the sort of man to change his opinion at a moment's notice.

'He is tough, ruthless, and as hard as granite,' she thought.

And yet, strangely enough, he read poetry and had spoken of 'An idealistic love which some of us seek.'

It was a strange thing to say, unless of course he had sought for love and either had never found it, or had lost it.

Perhaps that was the key to the puzzle of Magnus Fane.

"Idealistic love is, I believe, what Fleur has for Tim Sheldon," Delysia said aloud.

The task ahead of her however, was not to convince herself, but Magnus Fane, of the fact.

*   *   *

At luncheon they talked and argued about quite impersonal subjects. By dinner time the sea was considerably rougher.

"I am glad you have been to sea before," Magnus Fane said as the meal ended, "otherwise I should have to warn you not to be thrown about and risk breaking your leg, or at the least being badly bruised."

"I am not going to boast in case it is unlucky," Delysia replied, "but I have been in a rougher sea than this."

"However I think it would be wise," he said, "for you to go to bed and read your books. We shall arrive at about noon tomorrow and we will be in calmer waters for the last hour or so of the journey."

Delysia waited, hoping he would tell her where that would be, but he appeared to have nothing more to say, and she rose from her chair and a little unsteadily left the Saloon.

She had the feeling it had been from her point of view a quite successful evening, but she could not be sure.

He was so overwhelmingly self-confident, so completely controlled, that she thought he was an enigma which the most astute man, let alone woman, would find hard to read.

He had looked very smart at dinner in his evening-clothes.

At the same time once again she was sure they were not of any particular importance to him.

He was certainly not like the Gentlemen she had met at Fleur's party whose cravats were so high that it seemed difficult for them to move their necks.

Nevertheless he was so good-looking in a strange, rather awe-inspiring way, that she was sure if he was seated at the head of a dining-table it would be impossible to notice any other man in the room.

"Perhaps it is his personality," she reasoned.

She remembered how she had once talked to her father about that magnetic quality of leadership.

"What is it," she had asked, "that makes men follow a General like the Duke of Wellington, or an Admiral like Lord Nelson?"

"There is an aura about them," Sir Kendrick had replied. "And they have a force, a power which is difficult to describe, but it is something that emanates from them and to which men are irresistibly drawn."

He had laughed as he spoke, but Delysia had known what he meant.

Now as she thought of Magnus Fane she knew he had that same power, and that was why people were afraid of him, or thought of him, as Fleur had, as the Demon King or an Ogre.

"He is very, very frightening," she told herself as she got into bed, "but for Fleur's sake I will not let him defeat me."

Then with a smile she opened the book he had lent her and thought however strange and intimidating her position might be, it had its moments of enjoyment.

Chapter Five

DELYSIA FELT THE YACHT come to a standstill and ran to the porthole.

Outside it was difficult to see anything but what she thought were the tops of trees.

They had sailed some distance northwards, and because they had been in fairly smooth water for the last hour she guessed, although she was not sure, that they were in the Wash.

She repacked everything she had taken out of Fleur's trunk, and one of the stewards having knocked at the door came in to put a strap round it before he took it away.

Delysia had the uncomfortable feeling that she was being taken to some place that would be frightening and which she would hate.

But she was determined not to give Magnus Fane the satisfaction of knowing that she was afraid.

She therefore held her chin high as she walked up the companionway onto the deck.

Then she saw as she had expected that the yacht was in a wide piece of water and she was certain it was part of the Wash.

Now she could see there were trees and amongst them she thought she had a glimpse of a building.

However before she had time really to look around Magnus Fane was beside her.

He moved towards the gang-plank which led onto a small wooden quay, and as they stepped ashore Delysia glanced at him and thought he looked grim.

There was in fact, none of the friendliness he had extended towards her yesterday when they had talked of other things rather than the fact that she was his prisoner.

Once ashore, she realised that there was no carriage waiting for them, and Magnus Fane started to walk up a rough path which led them away from the water-side towards the trees.

They had not gone far before Delysia was aware that what she had glimpsed was actually a Castle, and she knew that this was where Magnus Fane intended to imprison her until Tim Sheldon was safely married.

Because she had read a great deal of history she was sure it was one of the fortresses that had been erected originally along the east coast of England as a defence against the Vikings.

It was rather fascinating to think it had stood there for so long, and she felt a dozen questions come to her lips.

But because Magnus Fane had not spoken to her since they had arrived, she was determined not to reveal her curiosity.

They walked on and now she could see the Castle clearly.

Built of grey stone, it had a formidable appearance that made its impact as awe-inspiring as that of its owner.

There was a tower on one side with arrow-slits which proclaimed its age, but the rest of the building had obviously been added on at later dates.

The windows were large and the architecture while austere was quite attractive.

As they drew nearer still, to Delysia's surprise, there was a well-kept garden surrounding the foot of the Castle where the shrubs were in bloom.

They seemed almost a frivolous contrast to the cold severity of the grey stone building.

A few more steps and Delysia was aware that the front door, of oak with brass hinges and heavily studded, was open.

Several servants were waiting for their arrival.

She wondered if they were as apprehensive at seeing their master as she was at being with him, and she thought as he strolled along by her side that he was in fact, quite as awe-inspiring as Fleur had described him.

Then, just before they were within ear-shot of the staff waiting for them, Magnus Fane asked:

"I am waiting to hear what you think of my Castle."

Without considering, as spontaneously as if she was speaking to her sister, Delysia replied:

"It is very appropriate for the Demon King!"

Even as the words left her lips she saw him look down at her sharply and feared she had been very indiscreet.

"So that is what you call me!" he said after a moment.

"It is the way you have been described to me," Delysia corrected.

He gave a sharp laugh before he said:

"Perhaps it is in the circumstances, if you are thinking of yourself as the captive Princess. But let me assure you, in this story there will be no Prince Charming to come to your rescue."

Delysia wanted to ask defiantly how he could be sure of that.

Then she had to admit to herself he was speaking the truth. There would be no rescue as far as she was concerned, but only a terrifying confrontation when Magnus Fane discovered that he had been deceived!

In a way, it would be a satisfaction to make him look a fool.

At the same time she knew, if she was honest, that she was frightened of his anger, and it was not a pleasant thought to know that she would have to face it with nobody to support her.

She reached the front door and an elderly servant with grey hair came forward to say:

"Welcome Sir. I hope you've had a good journey here and the sea wasn't rough."

"Not uncomfortably so," Magnus Fane replied.

He walked into the hall which contained a huge open fireplace in which a log was burning brightly.

There were several portraits on the walls and Delysia wondered if they were Fane ancestors, or if in fact,

Magnus Fane had bought the Castle 'lock, stock and barrel,' from its original owner.

He walked ahead of her into a room on the other side of the Hall which was far more attractive than she had expected, and was extremely well furnished with windows looking out towards the sea.

She was sure it could be cold and bleak in the Winter, but for the moment there was sunshine and Spring flowers in vases.

Again there was a large fireplace which was burning logs.

"Luncheon will be ready in ten minutes, Sir," she heard the servant say.

Then as he shut the door Magnus Fane walked to a table in a corner of the room on which there was a number of decanters and glasses.

She could see now that it was a very masculine room with large comfortable armchairs, and instead of china-cabinets which were fashionable in a Lady's Sitting Room, there were shelves filled with books.

Because she felt she had to know the answer Delysia asked:

"Is this your own house and where you live when you are in England?"

"It belonged to my uncle," Magnus Fane replied, "who because he had no children left it to me when he died. I spent a great deal of my childhood here, and as it is so isolated, I thought it a convenient place to bring you!"

She thought he was deliberately making himself unpleasant and sat down in a chair by the fire.

He turned to look at her from the drinks-table to ask:

"Would you like a glass of sherry? Or would you prefer a Madeira?"

"Madeira, please," she answered, "but only a very little."

He brought a glass to her and she took a sip before she said:

"I think this Castle is situated beside the Wash."

"You are quite right."

Delysia thought with a little sigh that she was a long way from London and she wondered, even if she could escape, how long it would take her to return to anything that was familiar and where she would feel safe.

As if he read her thoughts Magnus Fane said:

"There is no possible way by which you can evade me, so you had better settle down quietly. As you like reading, I can supply you with any number of books."

As he spoke he was standing with his back to the fire, a glass in his hand, and Delysia looked up at him to ask:

"How long are you thinking of keeping me here?"

"I have told you the answer to that already," he replied. "Until my nephew is married, as he is in honour bound, to the extremely suitable girl to whom he is engaged."

"But surely you intend to be at the wedding yourself?" Delysia asked. "How could they possibly manage without you?"

She was speaking provocatively, and she thought for a moment there was a slight twitch at the corners of Magnus Fane's lips as if he was amused by her defiance.

"I think it is more important," he replied, "to make sure that you do not entice Tim from his path of duty. As soon as he becomes a bridegroom I will have you conveyed back to London where doubtless a number of your ardent admirers will welcome you with open arms."

Now he was being deliberately sarcastic, and as Delysia could not think of anything particularly witty or even rude to say, she remained silent.

Then sharply, in the voice he had used to her when they first met, Magnus Fane said:

"Make no mistake, I intend to keep you here and there is nothing you can do about it!"

"You are only provoking me into retorting that I shall try," Delysia replied lightly.

"I suppose if you swam back the way we came you might have a chance," Magnus Fane answered. "Or, alternatively, if you suddenly developed wings or had the use of a balloon, you might get away. But I would advise you against any such ideas as you may have of thwarting me."

Delysia laughed and she knew the sound surprised him.

"I am laughing," she explained, "simply because the whole situation is so ridiculous!"

"I do not know why you should say that!"

"But you must see that you should have something better to do than to waste your brain, your ingenuity, and your determination in preventing your nephew from finding happiness, and to take so much trouble over one unimportant and weaponless young woman!"

"Not pistols and swords, Miss Langford," Magnus

Fane replied, "but weapons far more subtle, and in my opinion where a young and impressionable man is concerned, very much more dangerous."

"I suppose I should take that as a compliment," Delysia said, "but actually, if you want the truth, I think you are behaving in a surprisingly brainless manner."

She knew as she spoke that she was being insulting, but she did not care.

She felt that Magnus Fane was far too puffed up with his own consequence and far too sure of himself.

For the moment she was not afraid, she only thought what a triumph it would be when he found out that he had made a fool of himself.

She felt he was waiting for her to offer an explanation of her last scathing remark.

"All I can say is that you must have a very poor opinion of your nephew. After all, with a mind of his own, he is a man. Yet you insist on his living with a woman whom he mistakenly, and because he was pressured into it, asked to be his wife."

She looked up at him as she went on:

"Surely you must realise that you are asking him to accept meekly, subserviently, what is bound to be a disastrous marriage? To be brave enough to tell the truth is the behaviour of a man worthy of the name."

Magnus Fane laughed, but it was a sound that had no humour in it.

"Bravo, Miss Langford!" he said. "That is very plausible! At the same time, because I am convinced that you are quite incapable of making any man, let alone my nephew, happy, you can put forward no argument which will make me change my mind!"

"Do you really consider yourself capable of judging something that is so exclusively personal to the people concerned?"

"The answer to that is 'yes'!" Magnus Fane replied. "There are certain standards of behaviour that any decent man will expect from his wife, and you, Miss Langford, conform to none of them!"

His voice sharpened as he continued:

"As I have already said, what I have learnt about you and your behaviour convinces me absolutely that Tim would soon bitterly regret having married you, probably after only a few months!"

He spoke in a lofty manner and so positively that Delysia felt her temper rise and longed to rage at him.

But she knew that to do so would be to play into his hands and make him all the more convinced that Fleur was an uncontrolled, irresponsible young woman who indulged in one mad escapade after another.

She therefore sat very still.

Then after taking one more sip from her glass she put it down on one of the small tables near to her.

"I expect now you would like to see your bedroom," Magnus Fane said, as if he felt, as she had, that there was no more to be said on the subject under discussion.

"Thank you."

She rose to her feet and followed him to the door. Then before he turned the handle he said:

"Let me assure you once again that there is no escape from the bedroom which I have chosen for you. At the same time, in case you should think of trying anything so foolhardy, the door will be locked at night. I would also point out that there is a thirty-foot drop from the window, and to clamber out of it would merely mean that you would break your neck!"

"How kind of you to warn me!" Delysia said.

"I have already been told that you have an unusual head for heights," Magnus Fane replied. "In fact, Lady Winterton was very voluble about how you dared her son to follow you along a high wall from which he unfortunately slipped and fell, breaking his leg."

For one second Delysia was almost surprised into saying that she had never heard of Lady Winterton.

Then she realised this must be another of Fleur's escapades which had doubtless been blown up and exaggerated and made to sound far more reprehensible than it really was when it was reported to Tim's uncle.

She did not therefore tell him that she was, in fact, terrified of heights.

She remembered however that Fleur had been quite fearless when she was small and had climbed up onto the roof of the house and to the tops of the trees while she herself merely watched her sister.

She had actually been far too nervous to climb even to the top of a ladder, but she said nothing as Magnus Fane opened the door and walked with her to the foot of the stairs.

"My housekeeper, Mrs. Barrow, will show you to your room," he said.

Without looking at him Delysia walked slowly up the stairs to where an elderly woman in black silk with the chatelaine at her waist was waiting for her.

The bedroom was, as she might have expected, on

the second floor and although it was extremely well-furnished and the large canvas wooden bed looked comfortable it looked from the point of view of escaping to offer no hope.

To her surprise the turret on one side of it had been arranged as a dressing-room, and on the other side there was a comfortable Boudoir with a small book-case containing a number of shelves filled with books.

She was quite certain they had not been selected especially for her, but were what Magnus Fane would consider necessary for the comfort of any guest he invited to his home.

"Do you wish to change your gown, Miss, before luncheon?" the Housekeeper asked.

"No, thank you," Delysia replied.

"There's a can of hot water in the Turret Room, Miss," the Housekeeper went on, "but is there anything else you'd like before the maids have time to unpack your trunk?"

"I cannot think of anything, thank you."

She tidied her hair. Then with a last look round the bedroom she walked demurely down the stairs.

Magnus Fane was waiting for her in the hall and they moved side by side into what she realised was a Baronial Dining Room.

It was already part of the old house when doubtless a large family were living there and the Lords of the Manor entertained royally in that isolated part of the country.

Because she was curious she could not help asking:

"Do you look forward to coming here after having been in the East?"

"I suppose if I am honest," Magnus Fane replied, "I always think of the Castle as 'home,' and it is where I expect to retire to when I am old."

"You have a long time to wait for that, and meanwhile your staff must find it very lonely here with nobody to wait on."

There was a little pause before Magnus Fane said almost reluctantly:

"I send friends to stay here from time to time who have been ill or want to get away and rest from their responsibilities."

Delysia realised that this was why the house looked so 'lived-in,' and she said:

"That is kind of you."

"Even a Demon King can have his moments of generosity!"

"Except where I am concerned!" Delysia retorted.

He raised his eyebrows and she explained:

"I consider it very ungenerous not to offer any opportunity to defend herself to somebody whom you have accused of a number of crimes, or to consider any extenuating circumstances which are always there, if one looks for them and listens."

"I am not interested in listening to your pleas for mercy, if that is what you are intending to offer me," Magnus Fane replied. "So I suggest we change the subject and talk about something else."

Once again he made Delysia angry and she knew she hated him for the way in which he was condemning Fleur entirely on hearsay.

She kept wondering who it could have been who had prejudiced him so bitterly against her sister that he refused to listen to even the most reasonable arguments, or to deviate in any way from his complete and utter condemnation of her.

When luncheon was finished Magnus Fane suggested that they go to the stables.

Delysia walked with him to where on the other side of the trees there were commodious stables.

She expected he would have good horses and with her first glance she knew that those she was seeing were in fact, exceptional.

She soon learned that the majority of the animals had arrived only two days previously from the South.

"They did not find the journey too hard?" she heard Magnus Fane ask the Chief Groom.

"Not they, Sir. The lads brought 'em along nice an' steady, as you ordered, an' they've settled down well, as you'll find when ye rides 'em."

Magnus Fane smiled.

"What could be better than now?"

"I'll 'ave one saddled an' brought to the front door in five minutes, Sir," the groom said. "Will th' Lady be ridin' too?"

This was something that had not entered Magnus Fane's head and he looked at Delysia before he asked:

"Would you like to ride?"

"I should love it," she replied.

"Very well, bring two horses in ten minutes!" Magnus Fane ordered and started to walk back to the house.

Because she was excited Delysia could not help saying:

"Thank you! Thank you! I love riding more than anything else in the world, and I can see that your horses are exceptional!"

"I have a friend who exercises them for me when I am away from England," Magnus Fane explained. "I also have as it happens, quite a number of horses in training in Calcutta."

After what he had said Delysia was not surprised to find that he rode magnificently, just as well as her father did.

But if he had not surprised her, she knew that he was definitely surprised when he saw the way she could ride.

Although Fleur was a good rider, she did not have the passion for it that Delysia had, and she imagined therefore that nobody would have bothered to comment about it to Magnus Fane.

But as they had both ridden almost since the moment of leaving the cradle, there would be few women in London who could compete with either of them.

'He has been far too busy listening to all Fleur's misdemeanours in London,' Delysia thought bitterly, 'to hear about the country pursuits she enjoys, and what a different character she is from what he believes her to be.'

Now, because she was on a horse and the sun was shining, it was difficult not to enjoy herself as herself, while she galloped beside Magnus Fane.

As they jumped one or two low fences she was thinking that perhaps her enforced imprisonment might not be as unpleasant as she had at first anticipated.

She thought however that while he appeared to relax a little while they were riding over the countryside and was as charming as he had been the day before, yet the moment they returned to the house it was as if a barrier had fallen between them.

She felt sure it was because he was afraid once again that she might somehow trick him and prevent Tim Sheldon from marrying the Duke of Dorset's daughter.

However, knowing it would be a mistake to be continually bickering with him, she forced herself to congratulate him on the Castle, his horses, and his books.

She had thought as she came down from her bedroom that it would be more sensible to forget, for at least a little while, the 'bone of contention' which lay between them and which made every other sentence seem to have a barbed meaning.

All the gowns in Fleur's trunk were expensive and very beautiful, and Delysia found it difficult to decide which she should wear.

In the end, it was the Housekeeper who decided for her by saying:

"I'm hoping, Miss, as you'll wear this very pretty pink gown. The colour'll cheer up the darkness of the walls and make you look like a flower."

"Thank you," Delysia replied.

"It's a pleasure, Miss, to have somebody as young and pretty as yourself here. The Master's friends are usually old gentlemen, and while we enjoys looking after them, it's not the same as having somebody like you."

Delysia knew that because she was wearing Fleur's gown which was far more expensive and more elegant than anything she herself owned, it gave her a confidence she might not otherwise have had.

She was smiling as she walked down the stairs and into the Sitting Room.

But one look at Magnus Fane's expression told her that he was still in his grim mood, determined to hate her, determined to keep pointing out her faults.

Because it was a challenge she decided to circumvent him.

As soon as they sat down to dinner she said:

"Will you think it inquisitive if I ask you how you have managed, though you are still quite young, to make yourself not only so wealthy and so important in the East, but also so feared?"

As if the question took him by surprise Magnus Fane laughed.

"If that is my reputation, I shall not quarrel with it."

"Tell me your secret."

"Hard work!"

"There must be more to it than that!"

He hesitated, and she felt he was either feeling for words, or had decided not to answer.

Then she said:

"I think perhaps you use your perception, which is something I have always heard is part of Eastern thinking."

"You are right, although I would not have put it quite in those words," Magnus Fane said.

"Then what would you call it?"

"I suppose really it is a determination to find out the truth, which means looking deep into another person's heart and perhaps, although it sounds somewhat exaggerated, to read their thoughts."

Delysia gave a little cry.

"That is what I have always believed, and it is what I call 'perception,' because that is how I have thought of it ever since I was a child."

"And how do you use this 'perception'?" he asked.

She felt from the way he spoke that he was sure she was putting on an act just to interest him, but because she was anxious to prove him wrong she said:

"I am sure that you are an expert at looking deep into somebody to find out, as you said, the truth. But when I look deep into you, I am surprised!"

"Surprised? In what way?"

"Because you are far more vulnerable than you admit, and far more sensitive than anybody gives you credit for."

Delysia had for the moment forgotten that she was pretending to be Fleur. She was speaking as herself while using her perception, as her mother had taught her to do when she was a child.

"Do not only see things that are on the surface, dearest," she had said once. "When people tell you something, try to understand their motives for what they are saying. Try to sense if they have a reason, like unhappiness, fear, or perhaps just love, for saying or doing something which is different from what you expect."

For the moment she felt that Magnus Fane was not the Demon King that Fleur had told her he was, but rather a man who was battling in his own life against a great deal of opposition and was succeeding in his aims by using a force that was greater than himself.

At the same time, he was still an ordinary man

with the same feelings as anybody else, and not merely an autocrat who gave orders and expected them to be obeyed.

The thoughts flashed through her mind. Then she said:

"I think that sometimes, when you count up how much you have gained materially, you are disappointed in what you have achieved spiritually."

She spoke very quietly, then she added as if to herself:

"I am sure that living in the East has made you more conscious that things of the spirit are necessary to you than you would have been if you had lived only in England."

As she finished speaking she saw that Magnus Fane was staring at her, an expression of sheer astonishment in his eyes.

Abruptly he asked:

"Who has told you this? Who has been talking to you about me?"

His sharp tone brought Delysia back from a kind of Dreamland in which she had been thinking of him rather than of herself, and he saw the flush of colour in her cheeks before she said:

"Nobody...I have discussed you with no-body...except that I was told you were a cross between a Demon King and an Ogre, and that you frighten everybody who knows you."

She felt he was not convinced and she went on:

"What really surprised me when I first saw you was that you were so young. I had visualised a very old man with white hair."

"The other things you have said—have you thought them out for yourself?"

"I was putting my own thoughts into words."

Magnus Fane did not say anything. He merely drank a little of the claret by his side, then put down his glass, remarking dryly as he did so:

"You have surprised me, Miss Langford, but I suppose reading so widely has put ideas into your head which I have not found in any other ladies with whom I have dined."

"I cannot believe, Mr. Fane, that you have dined with many ladies who are young or in the extraordinary circumstances in which we find ourselves!"

"I suppose that is true," he admitted.

"Has it occurred to you, Mr. Fane," Delysia went on, "that if anybody learnt where I was at this moment, they would be very shocked to know that you have not provided me with a chaperon!"

She knew as she spoke that the idea that she needed one had never entered his head.

"Not that it matters," she continued, "for I imagine the fewer people who learn of your unconventional behaviour the better. At the same time, I hope, Mr. Fane, that my father does not ever become aware that I have been forced into accepting such a compromising situation."

Magnus Fane did not speak and Delysia thought with a feeling of amusement that she had caught him at a disadvantage and left him without any means of defending himself.

Then as if he felt he must say something, he remarked:

"I can only hope, Miss Langford, for your sake, that my nephew will be married, as I have suggested, as quickly as possible. Then you can return to the life you enjoy and which you are undoubtedly missing here in the wilderness."

"I am not complaining, Mr. Fane," Delysia replied. "In fact, I was anticipating as you know, a far more unpleasant prison than you have chosen for me."

She paused before she went on:

"However we were, if you remember, talking about perception, and I was just pointing out to you that your perception about people and about certain situations, is not infallible."

She thought as she spoke that she had scored another point for Fleur, which would perhaps make him think that some of the opinions he had formed about her sister were mistaken.

To her surprise he turned towards her and said very quietly:

"As we are being frank with each other, suppose you tell me honestly and truthfully why you have behaved as you have?"

There was a pause before Delysia asked:

"In what way?"

"You know to what I am referring. The life you lead, your behaviour with a large number of other men before you started to concentrate on my nephew."

Delysia did not speak and he asked:

"Do you really care for him? Or was it just because he was engaged to somebody eminently suited for him, and out of pure devilment you decided to take him away from her?"

Delysia stiffened. Then she said angrily:

"That is a monstrous thing to say! How can you believe that I could do anything so wicked as to deliberately break up an engagement, or a marriage between two people if they were happy?"

The words seemed to ring out in the large Dining Room.

Then in a lower tone she said:

"I should have thought that the perception you have used in the past and which has won so much for you would have told you the truth."

"Which is?"

"That love knows no barriers, no bounds, and cannot be constrained. Even you must acknowledge that!"

"I do not acknowledge it!" Magnus Fane said. "For people who are self-controlled and who wish to behave honourably, love is not a sufficient excuse for doing what is wrong and antisocial."

"That is where you are mistaken."

"Perhaps in your opinion, Miss Langford, but not in most people's."

"Most people do not find what they seek in life, either materially or spiritually. If you begin to look deeper and with more perception than you are using at the moment, you will find what every man and every woman really requires, longs for, and yearns for, is quite simply to find love."

"You are wrong, completely and absolutely wrong!" Magnus Fane said aggressively.

Delysia did not reply. She merely shook her head.

After a moment, as if he must reassure himself, Magnus Fane said:

"I shall prove you wrong, and I hope you will have the honesty to admit it when my nephew marries the woman to whom he is engaged and shuts you out of his life."

Chapter Six

As if what she had said upset him, Magnus Fane was more disagreeable than he had ever been before, and certainly more grim.

He spoke only in monosyllables until Delysia went to bed, where she lay awake in the darkness thinking what a strange man he was.

Yet at the same time it was fascinating to be able to duel with anybody so formidable, and to know that occasionally she scored points on Fleur's behalf which if he was honest he could not deny.

The next morning she received a message to say that as he would be busy until luncheontime he would be obliged if she would keep to her Sitting Room and not come downstairs.

The message also informed her that he had ordered horses for two o'clock.

That was some consolation!

At the same time, as Delysia had not previously been confined to her own rooms she felt constricted and really imprisoned, which made her angry.

However there were books to read, and she knew she would enjoy them.

Even so, she was acutely aware that the sun was shining outside and she wanted to be out in the fresh air.

She also in some way she could not determine for herself resented the fact that Magnus Fane was leaving her alone and was more interested in the other things he had to do.

At least until now he had been with her during her captivity, almost all the hours of daylight and, although she hated to admit it, she missed him.

She opened the window and leaned out, feeling the salt breeze on her face.

She thought how centuries ago other women like herself must have looked out from this same window dreading the sighting of the strangely shaped Viking ships coming towards them, intent on plundering everything they possessed.

It made her wonder if it was worth fighting for one's possessions, and whether Magnus Fane valued his so much that he would risk his life for them.

It was a question she wanted to ask him and she thought of several more which she was certain would involve a discussion at luncheon.

When she went downstairs having now been told by a servant that he was waiting for her, she was aware that his mood was still grim, and she did not like the expression in his eyes when he looked at her.

She felt he was scowling at her like the Demon King, thinking up some worse punishment he could inflict upon his victim.

However she told herself she was being imaginative and set out to try to entertain him at luncheon, making provocative remarks which she felt must bring forth some response.

She had to admit however that by the time the meal, which was only a short one, was finished, Magnus Fane was still as aloof and unresponsive as he had been when they started.

She had thought it wise in order to save time to have luncheon in her riding-clothes.

Fortunately in Fleur's trunk there had been a very attractive habit that she must have bought to ride in Rotten Row.

Of heavy blue silk it was trimmed with white braid, and to wear under it was a light lawn blouse inset with lace.

It was obviously very expensive and Delysia wondered what her father would say when he received the bill.

At the same time, she was glad to have anything so fascinating to wear, and she only regretted that the high-crowned hat with the gauze veil which would have matched it had been left behind.

However she arranged her hair as neatly as possible and thought that as far as she was concerned, it was pleasant to feel the warmth of the sun on her skin.

She had left her gloves in the hall and one of the servants had put beside them a small whip which she had borrowed the previous day when they went riding.

She picked them up, and by the time she had done

so Magnus Fane had walked ahead of her through the front door and down the steps to where the horses were waiting.

Instead of assisting her into the saddle as he should have done, he mounted his own horse, a large black stallion, and rode ahead as if he was impatient.

She thought it rude and deliberately spent more time than she need have done in seeing that her skirt was properly arranged over the stirrup.

He had in consequence, ridden quite some way before she caught up with him.

She was mounted on a different horse today—a much more spirited animal.

She supposed the Head Groom had seen how well she rode and had chosen this one for her knowing she would prefer it to anything more docile.

The horse was certainly skittish, tending to shy at a falling leaf and occasionally bucking, not in a vicious way but merely playfully.

Delysia told herself as she got the animal under control that it was a pity its Master was so much more difficult and definitely uncontrollable.

As if he was determined to be contrary, Magnus Fane rode in a different direction from the way they had taken before.

Delysia had been looking forward to jumping the hedges that might almost have been arranged as a private race-course.

They passed through some fields planted with young wheat and came to open ground where the hedges were very high and had obviously not been trimmed during the winter.

As if the sight of them angered Magnus Fane, he

spoke for the first time and said crossly:

"I cannot think why these fields have been left so wild! I shall speak to my Manager about them tomorrow. We will have to find a gap in the hedge or a gate, unless we turn back."

Because she was annoyed with him for being so perverse and having deliberately ignored her overtures to be friendly at luncheon, Delysia said coldly:

"I see no reason to do that. I am sure these horses can manage to jump the hedge ahead without much difficulty."

"Nonsense!" Magnus Fane replied sharply. "It is much too high and I will not permit you to attempt it."

It was the manner in which he spoke rather than his words which made Delysia feel defiant.

She studied the hedge speculatively and was quite certain that although it was high it would present no real problem.

As he said the last words and did not expect to be contradicted, Magnus Fane began to turn his horse preparatory to returning the way they had come.

Without saying anything Delysia brought her whip down lightly on her mount and rode him forward.

There was just about the right amount of ground to cover before they reached the hedge and as if the horse knew exactly what was expected of him he took off with an eagerness which showed he was not in the least intimidated by its height.

They cleared the hedge with a few inches to spare.

But as they reached the other side of it, Delysia realised she had been somewhat rash.

The ground, instead of being firm as it was where

they had taken off, was soggy and soft, and as her horse's front hoofs sank into it he staggered and fell forward throwing her from the saddle.

She was not hurt and she had had very much worse falls in her life.

As she sat up her horse pulled his hoofs out of the mire and moved on.

It was then, just as she was struggling to her feet not particularly shaken but annoyed that she should have fallen off, she saw Magnus Fane jump the hedge a little further down.

As he rode towards her she turned her head to smile at him, ready to say that although she had fallen there were no bones broken, when the words seemed frozen on her lips.

Never had she seen a man look so angry and, because he was scowling, his eye-brows seemed almost to meet across his nose.

He dismounted leaving his horse free and walked the last steps towards her.

"Blast you!" he said furiously. "How dare you risk your life in that damnable manner!"

As he spoke he brought down the whip he held in his right hand sharply across her shoulders.

She gave a little scream of protest, and as she did so he threw his whip on the ground, pulled her roughly into his arms, and his lips came down on hers.

They were hard and brutal, and for a moment Delysia could not believe that what was happening was not a figment of her imagination.

The shock first of feeling the whip on her shoulders then the pain of his kiss, seemed to take away the power of thought and leave her helpless and bewildered, aware only that she had no defence against him.

She could feel his lips bruising hers, and yet it was impossible to struggle, impossible even to breathe.

Then, as if he became aware how soft and helpless she was, his kiss became more gentle and yet was still insistent, masterful and demanding.

Then as the darkness that had begun to cloud her mind was lifting, Delysia suddenly realised that she ought to struggle against him and save herself from his brutality.

Yet as she tried to move it was impossible, for he held her completely captive.

Now suddenly the agony had gone and instead there was something strange, and in an extraordinary way wonderful, moving within her breasts.

She could not explain it, she could not even consciously think of it, and yet it was there.

She could feel it seeping through her whole body, making her quiver until it touched her lips and seemed to belong to his.

Then as she tried to understand what was happening she realised that she was being kissed for the first time in her life, and it was very different from what she had ever imagined.

Magnus Fane released her.

"Damn you!" he said furiously. "You could drive any man to drink!"

Because she had great difficulty in keeping her balance and not falling to the ground, Delysia put out her hands to hold onto him, but he had gone.

He walked away from her, caught hold of his horse that was standing by hers contentedly cropping the grass, and swung himself into the saddle.

Without looking back he galloped away at a speed which took him out of sight almost before Delysia could realise what was happening.

Alone in the large empty field, she put her fingers up to her lips as if to reassure herself they were still there and that what had just occurred had not been part of some strange dream.

"He . . . kissed me!" she said to herself. "How dare he do . . . such a . . . thing?"

And yet she was not angry, only shocked, bewildered, but at the same time aware that he had evoked within her strange sensations she had never known before, which were half-pain and half-pleasure.

Slowly, as if she was walking in a dream, she moved towards her horse.

Because she had always ridden alone at home whenever her father could not accompany her, she had no difficulty in mounting without any help.

It struck her though, that most ordinary young women would have found it a difficult thing to do.

She rode slowly back towards the house, fearing yet hoping that she might see Magnus Fane on the way.

She felt that somehow he must make some explanation of what had happened.

However, when she tried to reason it out for herself, it all seemed too complicated to put into words.

He hated and despised her, thinking she was Fleur, and yet while he had struck her for disobeying him, he had kissed her because he had thought she had endangered her life.

It did not make sense, and she knew although she had been hurt and astounded by his kisses that she had not been repelled by them.

She could still feel that strange feeling within her breast which seemed to linger there and was, when she thought of it, almost a rapture, or what she believed rapture must be like.

"How could he do . . . that to . . . me?" she asked.

Then she remembered that he thought he was kissing Fleur.

It suddenly struck her that perhaps Magnus Fane was showing more violently than he had before, his contempt and dislike of the girl who he thought had enslaved his nephew.

And yet she was sure he had been angry because he was afraid that she had injured herself when she fell.

It was all so complicated and she felt, since they were bound to meet again, that she must force him into an explanation of why he had behaved as he had.

Then she knew that it would be very embarrassing to have to ask him to tell her why he had kissed her.

Riding over the field she knew she had never imagined that a man's lips could be so hard.

Once again she put up her fingers to touch her mouth.

As she did so she felt a strange little quiver run through her, almost like a streak of lightning.

She knew that too had been part of the sensation she had felt when his kiss grew more gentle.

She wondered what Fleur would have done in the same circumstances.

Perhaps as Fleur had been kissed before, as she

never had, it would have presented no problems, and she might indeed have surprised Magnus Fane by kissing him back.

'I do not understand what it means,' Delysia thought miserably.

She rode on, looking as she did so both to the right and to the left in case she should see Magnus Fane in the distance.

But there was no sign of him, and because she had no wish to jump again, it took her a long time to find a way out of the field and return the way they had come.

Only as she neared the Castle did she think perhaps the grooms would consider it very strange that she and their Master should return separately.

There was nothing she could do about that, and when she drew up at the front door a groom appeared immediately to take her horse from her.

She was too shy to ask him if Magnus Fane was already home.

Instead she went inside the hall, but could not see his hat or whip on any of the chairs, and suspected that he was still riding but on a different part of the estate.

She went up the stairs, conscious as she did so that she was a little stiff from her fall, but otherwise was quite unhurt by it.

An elderly maid came to her room when she rang to help her change and she put on one of Fleur's pretty gowns as the maid said:

"If you're going out again, Miss, I think you should wear a coat. There's a wind coming from the sea that makes me think we'll have a storm afore nightfall."

"Oh, I hope not!" Delysia said automatically.

"The weather's very changeable at this time of the year," the maid replied. "What I'll do, Miss, is to put your coat and the scarf you wear on your head, in the hall, so that it'll be there if you need it."

"Thank you," Delysia said. "That would be very kind."

She finished dressing and went into the Boudoir next door wondering if Magnus Fane was back.

She sat down in a chair and reasoned with herself.

If she were really fast or improper as he supposed Fleur to be, he would not expect her to be disappointed or even angry when he kissed her.

She felt a little quiver go through her at the thought of what his kisses entailed.

Then she went on almost as if she was setting it all down on paper:

"The best thing I can do is to act naturally and pretend that nothing unusual has happened. He should of course apologise to me, but I am certain he will do nothing of the sort!"

She looked at herself in the gold-framed mirror and knew that, while Fleur's gown was very attractive, and her hair was well arranged, her eyes seemed unnaturally large.

What was worse, there was a look of fear in their depths which she could not disguise.

"Of course I am afraid of him!" she said angrily as if she had been accused of being a coward. "He is very frightening, and I am not used to people hating me and at the same time kissing me!"

She saw the colour come into her face as she spoke the words aloud and turned away impatiently.

She told herself she was old enough to be more sensible, and it would be ridiculous to make a scene over what had occurred.

She thought of going downstairs to wait for Magnus Fane to return, then had the uncomfortable feeling that if she tried to do so, the servants would stop her.

It was humiliating enough to have her room locked at night, and she knew unless she was with him she was expected to keep to her own Sitting Room.

She therefore went into the next room and found a book she had thought would be absorbingly interesting, but somehow she could not concentrate on it.

Her thoughts kept straying back to the strange way in which Magnus Fane had behaved when she had fallen from her horse.

She sat thinking for such a long time that she suddenly realised that the sun had disappeared and it must be getting late.

The door opened and Delysia looked up quickly, only to see that the maid was standing there.

"Your bath's ready, Miss!" she said.

"Is it time to dress for dinner?" Delysia enquired.

"It'll be ready in just over half-an-hour, Miss."

Because she knew it was a mistake to be late Delysia hurriedly took off the pretty gown she had put on and got into the bath which had been arranged for her in the Turret Room.

The water was scented and she wondered if the fragrance came from the Still Room of the Castle, or whether it had been bought.

She thought it was a question she might ask Magnus Fane, but was certain he would not be interested.

She took a great deal of time in choosing a becoming gown to wear, hoping it would in some way, placate him and knowing too that it gave her confidence in herself.

If she was honest, she was feeling not only apprehensive about meeting him again, but also very shy.

He had kissed her and it seemed a very odd thing for him to want to do, considering how much he hated and despised her.

She supposed that as the Demon King he had rules that he made for himself that were not the same as those to which other people conformed.

When she was ready she said to the maid:

"Shall I go downstairs?"

As she spoke there was a knock at the outer door and the maid crossed the room to speak to somebody outside.

Delysia could not hear what they were saying, but she had the feeling that it was something untoward.

The maid came back into the room.

"The Master's not yet returned, Miss, and they wondered in the Pantry if you want to wait for him, or have your dinner upstairs."

"I will wait," Delysia decided.

As she spoke she walked into the Boudoir next door and picking up the book, of which she had read fewer than two pages, sat down in a chair in front of the fire.

It seemed to her that she had sat there for a very long time before the maid came to the door once more to say:

"Excuse me, Miss, but the Master's returned and as it's so late and he wishes to have a bath after riding, he's ordered your dinner to be brought up to you here."

For a moment Delysia could only stare at her.

Then she knew there was nothing she could do but accept what she felt was an insult.

How dare Magnus Fane lock her away in her room as if she was a naughty child in a Nursery?

How dare he not make his apologies himself rather than send them by a servant!

Then she knew that what she was thinking or feeling would not be of the slightest interest to him.

There was nothing she could do but wait until two footmen came into the room to erect a small table in front of the fire and cover it with a white cloth, then bring her dinner in course by course.

She was offered wine to drink, but she refused it, and because she was both angry and at the same time apprehensive she found it difficult to eat, in fact had no appetite.

She had a feeling that this was the start of a new phase in their relationship, and he was deliberately shutting her away as his prisoner.

She would therefore no longer be able to talk to him or ride with him.

'I cannot bear it!' she thought.

When dinner was over and the footmen having taken down the table carried her tray from the room, she wondered what would happen if she followed them and went downstairs to confront Magnus Fane.

Suppose she asked him for an apology?

Perhaps it would be more clever to behave as if nothing had happened and merely to be as charming as she had tried to be yesterday.

She suddenly felt very young and inexperienced.

She knew so little about men, and yet she had the feeling that she was coping with one of the most difficult men any woman could find.

"What shall I do?" she asked, and wished she could talk to her mother about Magnus Fane, and ask her advice.

Time seemed to pass very slowly, and when she realised it was only ten o'clock she felt as if she had waited for many hours and it must be nearly midnight.

"He is obviously not interested in me any more," she told herself. "So instead of waiting for him like some unwanted 'wall flower,' the best thing I can do is to go to bed!"

She felt this was a good idea not only because of what had happened with Magnus Fane, but also because she was still feeling stiff after her fall, and if she was honest—rather tired.

She knew she had not yet recovered from the exhaustion she had suffered after her father's illness, and she had certainly not, as the Doctor had expected, recuperated light-heartedly in London.

Instead she had been through one traumatic experience after another, and perhaps what had happened today was the worst.

She rang for the maid to help her out of her evening-gown and put on one of Fleur's gossamer-fine lawn nightgowns inset with lace.

It was so beautiful that Delysia felt it was almost too good to be used as a nightgown.

Then she remembered that Fleur would have bought it to take with her on her honeymoon with Tim Sheldon.

Because it was so transparent she felt embarrassed even to sit at the dressing-table without having something more with which to cover herself.

As if she knew what she was thinking, the maid brought her the negligee which matched it.

That too was very thin and almost as transparent, but in addition to the lace which decorated it there were small bows of blue velvet ribbon.

Delysia felt a little more comfortable in it, and as she sat down in front of the mirror to start brushing her hair the maid lit two candles by her bed and asked:

"Is there anything else you need, Miss?"

"No, nothing, and thank you very much," Delysia replied. "Please call me at eight o'clock."

"Very good, Miss."

The maid went from the room and Delysia heard her turn the key in the lock.

She wanted to scream at the impertinence of being locked in by a maid, but she knew if she did so, nobody would hear her.

She wondered how Fleur would have coped in similar circumstances.

She felt that her sister would somehow have managed to climb out of the window and up onto the roof, or would have done something equally unexpected and brave which would have astounded Magnus Fane.

'I am too frightened, and perhaps too stupid, to do anything but just sit here and be humiliated,' Delysia thought.

She brushed her hair, as her mother had always insisted she should do, until it seemed to have an electricity in it, all of its own.

Then rising from the stool on which she had been

sitting, she blew out the lights on the dressing-table and walked towards the bed.

As she did so, she heard the key turn in the lock and the next second the door opened.

She stood still wondering what had been forgotten.

Then to her astonishment Magnus Fane came into the room.

He was wearing his evening-clothes with drain-pipe pantaloons which had been introduced by the King when he was Prince Regent.

But Delysia could see only the strange expression in his eyes which seemed menacing, but as there was only a little light from the candles by the bed, she thought she might be mistaken.

He stood just inside the room looking at her and after a moment she asked nervously:

"What is . . . it? What has . . . happened? Why are . . . you here?"

There was a twisted smile on his lips as he replied:

"I can see I am somewhat over-dressed."

As she spoke he pulled off his tight-fitting black coat and flung it down on a chair.

Beneath it he was wearing one of the fine lawn shirts introduced by Beau Brummel which was so transparent that Delysia felt she could see the muscles of his body move beneath it.

She stared at him in astonishment. Then she said:

"You should not be in my room . . . and I am going to bed!"

"I can see that," he replied with a twist of his lips as he moved towards her.

Instinctively Delysia put her hands up to the front of her negligee as if to hide her breasts.

She felt that he noticed the movement before he said:

"I decided while I was out riding that it is a mistake to try to fight the obvious. In other words, you have won!"

Delysia stared at him.

"I . . . I do not . . . understand."

"I think you do," he replied. "Ever since you came aboard *The Sea Lion* and since you have been here, you have been using every wile in your repertoire to captivate me, as you captivated so many other fools! Well, my dear, I capitulate! Why should I deny myself anything so desirable?"

As Delysia stared at him, trying to comprehend what he was saying, his arms went round her and he pulled her against him.

Then before she could struggle, before she could realise what he was about to do, his lips were on hers and he held her captive, as he had done earlier in the day in the field.

His kiss was not so rough or so brutal as it had been then, but his lips were still hard and demanding.

There was too, Delysia felt, something insolent, even contemptuous in the way he had just taken her in his arms when she had not expected it.

Then as she tried to struggle against him she felt a sudden fire on his lips that was different from anything she had known before.

It was a fire that seemed to burn its way from her mouth into her throat and to ignite a flame within her that was like nothing she had ever dreamed or imagined.

Now the sensations she had begun to feel when he

kissed her in the field seemed to multiply and intensify until the flame within her flickered higher and higher and she knew it came from him, and that his whole body was burning.

He kissed her until she felt as if she had no identity of her own and was just part of something uncontrollable which swept through them both.

Then as she found it difficult to think but only to feel that she was lost in a strange world which had no reality about it, he picked her up in his arms and carrying her to the bed, flung her down against the pillows.

As she gave a cry of surprise and fear he was lying on top of her.

Now he kissed her fiercely and demandingly, so that his lips seemed to sear first her mouth, then her skin.

He kissed the softness of her neck and pulling away the lace negligee his lips were on her shoulder.

It was as she felt his hands against her body that Delysia realised what was happening.

In sudden terror she struggled to free herself from him, crying out as she did so:

"No . . . please . . . no . . . !"

They were the first words she had been able to say since he had kissed her.

Now he raised his head for a moment to look down at her.

In the light from the candles she could see the fire in his eyes.

At the same time, there was a strange, almost cynical twist to his lips that she did not understand.

"Why pretend?" he asked. "The time for games is

over. This is what you wanted, and you will find, as undoubtedly you have found already, that one man is very like another!"

"I...I do not know...what you are...s—saying!" Delysia stammered. "You...must not...k-kiss me! Please...you must...go away!"

Magnus Fane laughed, but it was not a very pretty sound.

"How disappointed you would be if I did! Stop pretending, Fleur, and let us enjoy ourselves!"

"No, no!" Delysia cried. "This is...wrong...you know it is...wrong!"

"If you are afraid of losing Tim, let me tell you that you have lost him already. And although I have no intention of offering you marriage, as he was stupid enough to do, you will find I can be very much more generous than he can afford to be."

There was something in the way Magnus Fane spoke which swept away the fire which had been burning in Delysia and made her feel as if she had been drenched with icy cold water.

She suddenly understood, although it seemed incredible, what he intended.

With a cry of sheer horror she attempted to push him away from her.

"How can you...think of anything so... wicked...so wrong?"

Even as she spoke she knew that Magnus Fane was not listening and her hands felt as if she was trying to move a rock of granite.

Slowly he bent down towards her, crumbling her resistance, making his body imprison hers, so that she was crushed beneath him.

He gave a low laugh, and once again he was kissing the softness of her neck and his hand was pulling her negligee lower so that she heard it tear.

It was then she was really terrified and her fear was like a dagger striking through her.

She was aware of her helplessness, of how small and weak she was.

She felt him overwhelm her, not only physically but mentally, so that she had no significance and was utterly and completely helpless.

Because it was so frightening, like a child that was lost in the dark she felt the tears come into her eyes.

As the pressure of his lips increased she could feel his hand moving over the curves of her hip.

She gave a sudden scream—pleading:

"Please . . . I am . . . frightened and there is . . . nobody to . . . help me!"

She sounded very young and her voice had an unmistakable note of terror in it.

For a moment Magnus Fane was still and she went on:

"What you are . . . doing is . . . wrong . . . wicked . . . I do not know how to . . . stop you . . . please . . . listen to . . . me!"

The words were almost incoherent, but they made Magnus Fane raise his head and in the candlelight he looked down at her.

Tears were running down Delysia's cheeks and the expression in her eyes was that of a child who was confronted by something terrifying and inexplicable.

For a moment he stared at her, then as her lips quivered she whispered:

"Please . . . do not do . . . this!"

Slowly, so slowly that it seemed to her as if a century of time passed, he raised himself from where he had been lying on top of her, until he was sitting on the side of the bed.

He looked down at her as if to convince himself that she was real and not something he had just imagined.

Because he had crushed her it was impossible for her to move, and she only lay straight out, her head against the pillow, her shoulder bare, the torn lace of her negligee ragged against the curve of her breast.

"Please . . ." she whispered again, "please . . .!"

Because tears filled her eyes she could only see him through a haze.

Abruptly, so that it took only a second to realise what he was doing, he rose from the bed, picked up his coat, and walked towards the door.

He pulled it open and went out, slamming it shut behind him and there was only the sound of his footsteps going down the corridor.

For some minutes Delysia could not move.

Then she turned her face against her pillow and burst into a flood of tears.

She cried until she slept from sheer exhaustion.

Later when the candles had guttered low, feeling very cold she crept between the sheets where she lay shivering.

*   *   *

Delysia awoke slowly, feeling something unpleasant had happened, though for the moment she could not remember what it was.

She realised that the sun was shining through the cracks in the curtains of her windows and it was morning.

As the memory of last night flooded over her, she asked in a voice that did not sound like her own:

"How can he have...thought of...doing anything so...wicked?"

The question answered itself as she remembered that he had thought her to be Fleur.

Although she wanted to believe that her sister had never behaved in the way Magnus Fane imagined she had, she could not escape from the memory of hearing Tim Sheldon's voice in Fleur's bedroom.

She tried not to think of it, and yet it was impossible to dismiss it, and not to know what Magnus Fane, thinking her to be Fleur, had expected of her last night.

She put her hands over her eyes with the shame and humiliation of it.

At the same time she felt as if she had suddenly grown up.

Never had she dreamt that gentlemen behaved like that, or that they could burn with a fiery desire for a woman they did not like and for whom they had the utmost contempt.

That same fire had ignited flames within herself!

"How could I...do anything...so wrong?" she asked helplessly and did not know the answer.

She could not pretend that she had not soon responded to Magnus Fane's kisses or that he had not evoked in her sensations which were so extraordinary and so insistent that she had felt as if she belonged to him and no longer herself.

Now she could see him as if he was standing in front of her.

There was a sardonic twist to his lips, and she knew that while he kissed her he had despised her for what he believed was her immorality.

As she thought of it she felt as if she went down into a slough of despond so foul that she would never feel clean again.

"Oh, Mama," she prayed. "How could this . . . happen to me? How can I bear to . . . think that Fleur could do . . . what he assumes she did?"

She wanted to cry with the sheer humiliation of it, but as already her head was aching and her eyes felt heavy she forced herself not to give way to her unhappiness.

Instead she looked at the clock on the mantelpiece and realised it was very much later than she had expected.

She supposed the maid had let her sleep and she rang the bell for her breakfast.

Afterwards she got up and when she was dressed Delysia asked tentatively if Mr. Fane was in the Castle.

She knew that unless he was, it was unlikely she would be allowed to leave her Sitting Room.

"I'll find out, Miss," the maid replied.

She left the bedroom and Delysia felt despairingly that perhaps after what had happened last night Magnus Fane would go riding and deliberately leave her locked away.

"How can I talk to him? How can I ever . . . face him again?" she asked.

At the same time, the alternative was to be alone with her own thoughts, which was a no more pleasant prospect.

The maid came back into the bedroom.

"The Master's downstairs in the Sitting Room, Miss," she said, "and I think he's expecting you to join him."

Delysia took a deep breath.

She wanted to go downstairs, and yet at the same time she wanted to hide from Magnus Fane.

What could she say to him? How could they ever talk of what had happened?

Then her pride, which had always been a very positive part of her character, came to her rescue.

It was he who was at fault, whether he admitted it or not, and she would not be intimidated!

Slowly she went from the room and walked along the corridor to the top of the stairs.

As she reached them, she was aware of a sound of wheels outside the front-door.

The hall was built in a well-shape with a dome for a ceiling and Delysia could look down onto the ground floor.

There was only one footman in the hall who opened the front-door.

As he did so Delysia could see that there was a closed carriage drawn by four horses outside, and stepping out of it was a lady elegantly dressed with a feather-trimmed bonnet.

Delysia looked at her in surprise, wondering who she could be and if she was a casual caller or somebody whom Magnus Fane was expecting.

The Visitor hurried up the steps, walked in through the front door and merely said as she passed the footman:

"Where is your Master?"

She hardly waited to hear the man reply: "In the Drawing Room, M'Lady!" before she ran across the hall and opened the door of the Drawing Room herself.

Then as she disappeared inside Delysia heard her say in a high, hysterical voice:

"They are married! They are married, Magnus! You promised me you would prevent them from running away—together!"

The last word was almost inaudible.

Then as the footman hurried to shut the door behind the newcomer Delysia knew the lady must be Tim Sheldon's mother.

She gave a little gasp and felt that she could not face the explanations she would have to make.

It would be bad enough after what had happened to confront Magnus Fane, but to be interrogated by Lady Sheldon would be, she thought, utterly unbearable.

It was she who had pressurised her son into becoming engaged to the Duke of Dorset's daughter, and who had undoubtedly told Magnus Fane the lies about Fleur that he had believed to be true.

"I cannot... face it! I cannot... bear it!" Delysia told herself.

Then almost as if a voice was guiding and helping her, she knew what she could do.

She ran back into the bedroom to find it empty as

the maid was tidying the turret where she had bathed.

She pulled a smart fur-trimmed coat which had belonged to Fleur out of the wardrobe and put it on, and then opened a drawer in the dressing-table where she put her handbag.

In it was the money she had brought with her when she was kidnapped from her father's house in London which amounted to quite a considerable sum.

She had expected there would be bills to be paid if she stayed as she intended in the house, and also so that Fleur would not be ashamed of her, she wanted to buy some more sophisticated clothes than those she had worn in the country.

She put the bag over her arm and only pausing to pick up the blue chiffon scarf she wore over her head, she ran down the two flights of stairs to the hall.

The footman, having shut the door of the Drawing Room, had vanished, presumably, Delysia thought, to tell the Butler that Lady Sheldon had arrived.

There was therefore nobody to see her as she opened the front door, and ran down the steps to where Lady Sheldon's carriage was waiting.

As she put the chiffon scarf over her hair she said to the footman who was standing on the ground talking to the coachman:

"There has been an accident! Will you take me immediately to the village? I have to find the Doctor. Please drive as quickly as you can!"

Just for a moment the two servants looked at her in surprise.

Then the coachman picked up his reins and the footman hurriedly opened the door of the carriage.

"It is very urgent!" Delysia said as she stepped in.

The footman jumped up onto the box, and the horses moved off.

Only as they turned into the main drive and their pace increased did she look back through the small rear window of the carriage to see with a feeling of relief that there was nobody on the steps watching them go.

At the same time, she knew if Magnus Fane learnt that his sister's carriage had driven away he might be suspicious, and she would have little chance of eluding him for long.

She was aware from what had been said by the servants, and because she was sure Magnus Fane had deliberately never taken her through the gates at the end of the Park, that there was a village not far from the Castle.

She was not mistaken and when they reached the village and she thought the coachman would ask her where the Doctor lived, she put her head out of the window to say:

"Stop at the shop! I will enquire there where the Doctor is likely to be."

The shop was a small one with a bow-fronted window, and Delysia suspected it was the only one in the village which seemed to consist of a number of thatched cottages and a Norman Church.

As the carriage came to a standstill she opened the door and jumped out before the footman could get down to help her.

She walked into the shop and found a very old man behind the counter, serving a woman carrying a baby.

As she appeared they both turned to stare at her almost open-mouthed.

"Would you be very kind," Delysia said, "and tell me where is the nearest Posting-Inn?"

For a moment it seemed as if her appearance had struck the two people to whom she was talking, dumb.

Then at last the old man said in a quavering voice:

"'T'be a mile up th' road, Ma'am, on th' main 'ighway."

"Thank you very much!"

Delysia rushed out of the shop knowing she had left them something to gossip about which might soon reach the ears of Magnus Fane, and she would undoubtedly have to hurry.

Outside she said to the coachman:

"Please take me to the Posting-Inn which is a mile up the road on the main Highway."

The coachman touched his hat with his whip and once again the footman shut the carriage door after she had stepped inside, and they drove off.

* * *

Later Delysia was to reflect that luck had been with her in a most miraculous manner.

When she reached the Posting-Inn she thanked the two servants who had carried her there, gave them each a guinea, and told them to return to the Castle.

They seemed surprised that her desire for a Doctor had ended at the Inn.

At the same time they were too well-trained to ask questions, and only thanked her for her generosity and drove off.

She had been afraid that in such an isolated place there would be no conveyance to take her any further, but because it was on a main road, a Post-Chaise was available although she was informed that it was drawn by only one horse.

She hoped that, if she paid extra, she would be able to change into a Chaise drawn by two horses when she reached the next stage of her journey.

She did not conceal the fact that she was travelling to London because she felt it would be useless.

She was certain that once Magnus Fane learned of her escape he would naturally assume that was where she would go.

Her only hope therefore was to make her way first to her father's house in Park Street, and then home to the Country where perhaps he would have more difficulty in finding her.

As he had not heard her leave the Castle and nobody else had seen her go, it would not be until Lady Sheldon's coachman informed him of what had happened that he would be aware that she had left.

She also reasoned that if her luck held, since Lady Sheldon would undoubtedly stay for luncheon, her carriage would be taken to the stables without the Castle staff being aware that it had been taken to the village and back again.

'I have been lucky so far,' Delysia thought, 'and I can only pray that it continues.'

All she wanted to do was to get away and not be involved in what she felt would be an hysterical denunciation of her sister by Lady Sheldon and the rage of Magnus Fane when he realised that not only Fleur had outwitted him, but so had she.

"He is angry enough already," she told herself, "and I cannot imagine what he will say now!"

At the same time she could still feel the fire on his lips and the hard strength of his body as he lay on her.

'Perhaps he will be sorry he has been so cruel and unkind to me,' she thought, then was sure that was most unlikely.

She travelled all day, and after three changes of horses reached a large Posting-Inn late in the evening.

She could now go no further because it was almost dark, but Delysia thought with satisfaction that if Magnus Fane had left the Castle to pursue her, it would be impossible for him to catch up with her tonight.

She was aware the Landlord of the Inn was surprised that anybody so young should be travelling alone.

She explained that she had had a very urgent summons to return to London immediately and had not had time to arrange for anybody to accompany her.

"My lady's-maid is ill," she said, "and I have therefore been forced to make the journey alone, but I am sure I shall be quite safe here with you."

"That's true, Miss, but it's a long way yet to London," he replied.

He then, on Delysia's instructions, gave orders that whoever was driving the Post-Chaise next day, must be prepared to arrive as late as possible at the last Inn where they would change horses and to leave at dawn the following morning.

Because Delysia was so expensively dressed and prepared to pay for the best bedroom and a private parlour, her story was accepted.

As she had to repeat it over and over again she became, she thought with a little smile, word-perfect, and at each stop more convincing than she had been at the one before.

When they finally reached London in what she thought must be a record time, considering how few hours of sleep she had had on the journey, she felt more exhausted than if she had ridden the whole way.

She had enough money left to pay the driver of the Chaise, and her generous tip delighted him.

It was old Newman who opened the door to her and he was surprised to see her.

"Is Lady Matlock still here?" she asked.

"Oh, no, Miss," Newman replied. "Her Ladyship left two days ago an' a terrible time we've had tidying up after the last party Her Ladyship gave!"

He was so full of grumbles about what hard work it had been after what Delysia guessed had been a very rowdy party, that he did not seem concerned that she had returned alone.

It was only when the old Housemaid who had looked after her before came to attend to her that she had to answer questions as to why she had gone away so unexpectedly without taking any luggage with her.

"We didn't know what was happening, Miss, and that's the truth!" the Housemaid said. "First you leave, then Miss Fleur was gone before the household were awake. We couldn't believe it, we really couldn't!"

The way she spoke of her sister gave Delysia an idea.

"When Miss Fleur left, did she leave a note for me?" she asked.

"Oh, yes, she did, Miss!" the Housemaid replied. "She leaves it on the mat outside your door, not knowing of course, you'd gone."

"Where is it now?"

The maid walked to the mantelpiece and took the letter from behind a photograph frame.

"I puts it up here to be safe, Miss, but it's a good thing you mentioned it, otherwise I'd have forgotten it was there!"

Delysia was not listening.

She hoped that Fleur in the letter would tell her all she wanted to know, where they were to be married and where she and her husband were now hiding.

But she forced herself to wait until the Housemaid had left the room to bring her something to eat and drink.

She had had a very inadequate and hurried meal at the last Inn at which they had changed horses.

When she was alone she opened Fleur's letter.

It was a long one, and had obviously been written in great haste in pencil.

Dearest Delysia,

> *Please do not be Angry with Me when You read this, but Tim and I will have Run Away! We have to leave at once because the Demon King has forbidden Him ever to see Me again, and has ordered Him, as if He were a raw recruit, to marry His official Fiancée immediately.*
>
> *I know you will be upset that We did not let You into the Secret, but I thought*

143

You would be bound to tell Me not to do anything in a Hurry. But We have no time, if We are to be Married and live Happily ever after!

Tim had it all planned before He arrived this evening, and He told Me about it while Hugo was entertaining You. Then when You had gone to bed He helped Me to pack as many trunks as We could.

But as We are going to start our Honeymoon in Paris, He has promised to buy Me everything I need there.

Try to understand, Dearest, that I love Tim with all my Heart, as He loves Me, and it would be Impossible for either of Us to think of Marrying anybody else.

I know You were shocked by the way Beatrice Matlock is behaving with the Duke, but I had to leave Cousin Sarah who was intriguing to make Me marry the horrible Marquess, and had ordered Tim out of the House.

We had to meet Somewhere, and as the Duke was prepared to pay for the Servants, the Food and the Wine so that He could see Beatrice, it seemed sensible to come here, however irresponsible She might be.

Cousin Sarah had told Tim's Mother a lot of Wicked lies about Me, and She of course repeated them to the Demon King who in turn told Tim what She had said.

I know You will believe me when I

tell You that I have never, never in My whole life behaved like Beatrice Matlock, and Tim says He would never do anything so Wrong as to make me His until We are properly married.

I have been, I know, foolish in lots of ways, but it was such fun having so many Men running after Me and begging Me to Marry them. But I never cared for any of them except Tim, and I know there will never be Anybody else in My life.

Between us We have the most Precious thing in the whole world and Tim says his Uncle can keep His money as far as He is concerned, as We have everything which matters, besides enough money to live in the Country and have lots of Children.

Please, My Dearest and Most Beloved Sister, understand and stand up for Me when people say how fast and immoral I am! I swear to You on everything Holy and on Tim's head, which is the most Holy of all, that I have never done anything Worse than allow one or two rather stupid young Men to kiss me on the cheek, and Tim is the only Man who has kissed Me properly.

Because Tim is so determined that No-One shall stop Us from being legally Married, We are leaving here very early tomorrow Morning, before anybody is Awake, and driving straight to Chelten-

ham where Tim will ask Papa's permission for Him to marry Me.

I know Papa will say 'Yes' then No-One can suggest that the Marriage is not Legal, and I am not really Tim's Wife.

We are then going to France so that We shall not be here to hear all the Screams and Hysterics of Tim's relatives!

When it has all quietened down, be an Angel and write to Me, care of Tim's Bank, which is Coutts—No. 92, Rue de la Paix.

The Manager is the only Person who will know our Address, and We will not come Home until everything is quiet and pleasant. You know what I mean!

You have been so Kind and Sweet to Me all these years, and I know that Tim, when he knows You better, will love You as I do, and You will be the very first Person We will invite to come to stay with Us.

Bless you, Darling, and take care of Yourself.

> *Your Affectionate Sister,*
> *Fleur*

P.S. We cannot go to Sheldon Park until Tim's Mother has moved out. I do not suppose She will ever forgive Me, but that is Cousin Sarah's fault for telling Her such a lot of Wicked lies!

Delysia read the letter, then she gave a little cry of delight.

Her heart was singing with happiness, not only because Fleur was married to the man she loved, but also because the horrible things Magnus Fane had said about her were untrue.

Most important of all, what she had thought when she had heard Tim in her sister's room was mistaken and the knowledge of what was really happening was like the lifting of a stone from her heart.

They had just been *packing!*

She wanted to go down on her knees and thank God for restoring her faith and belief in her sister.

"How can I have been so stupid," she asked herself, "as not to have guessed that as Mama's child, Fleur would not do anything really wrong, any more than I would?"

Chapter Seven

"I HAVE ESCAPED!"

Delysia awoke and found the words on her lips.

Then with a little sigh she felt how tired she was and there was nothing interesting to wake up to or to do.

She was surprised at finding herself so listless: she felt almost as if she had ridden in the Grand National and lost the race, or had climbed to the top of the Himalayas and having reached it was disappointed.

"I am being ridiculous!" she told herself.

Then she sat up in bed and pulled the bell.

After some time had elapsed the Housemaid came in to say:

"I expects you wants your breakfast, Miss."

"That would be very nice," Delysia agreed.

"Mrs. Newman's cooking it, an' it'll be brought up as soon as it's ready."

The maid pulled back the curtains and as the sunshine came streaming in Delysia thought how beautiful the garden at the Castle would be looking.

It came to her mind that if Magnus Fane came to London he might feel it imperative to seek her out and tell her what he thought of her deception.

The idea that he might do so made her heart beat quicker, and she felt herself trembling.

She knew then that she must go away and she played with the idea of either going to Cheltenham to be with her father or else home to the country.

She had almost decided that she would go to Cheltenham when her breakfast was brought in by old Newman. He was puffing with the exertion of carrying it upstairs as he set the tray down by the bed.

"We thinks you'd be hungry, Miss," he said, "as you didn't have much to eat last night, but the eggs in London ain't the same as them you gets in the country."

"I am sure I shall enjoy them very much," Delysia smiled.

He shuffled from the room and to please him and his wife after they had taken so much trouble she ate the eggs and bacon.

But despite the scanty amount of food she had eaten the night before, she did not really feel very hungry.

The hot coffee however, made her more alert and she told herself that the sooner she left London the better.

She was just deciding whether she should take all the clothes she had with her to Cheltenham or whether she should leave some behind in case she decided to come back when the Housemaid appeared again with a letter in her hand.

"This has just arrived by post, Miss," she said.

Delysia's heart gave a leap as for one second she thought it might be from Magnus Fane.

Then she told herself she was being very foolish, for of course even if he had written to her, which he would not have done anyway, there would not have been time for a letter to arrive from the Castle.

One glance at it told her however that it was from her father, for she would have recognised his handwriting anywhere.

She opened the letter, leaning back against her pillows as she did so, as if she felt she needed their support, and read:

My Dear Delysia,

> *I hope you are having an enjoyable time in London, and of course you will know by this time that Fleur is married to Lord Sheldon.*
>
> *They came here to ask my permission, and although I think it regrettable, when he was already engaged to another woman, Fleur persuaded me that their only hope of happiness was to be together.*
>
> *They were married by Special Licence in St. Mary's Church, and I gave Fleur away, even though it was an effort, as I am still not feeling very well.*
>
> *My Doctors, however are pleased*

with my progress, and I am not finding Cheltenham as boring as I expected because I have met a very charming fellow-patient by the name of Lady Bowden.

We have our meals together and spend what free time we have from our treatments playing Piquet, and talking about mutual friends.

As soon as I am well enough to travel home she is coming with me to stay at the Castle. Her husband was killed at Waterloo and she is very lonely, which is understandable.

I hope you will find the time to write to me and tell me how you are enjoying yourself. I hope too that the horses are all right at home, but I expect I would have been informed if there was any trouble.

Take care of yourself, My Dear Daughter,

Your Affectionate Father,

Kendrick Langford.

Delysia read the letter through carefully and thought she was certainly not wanted at Cheltenham.

She had the feeling that, as she had always hoped, her father had found somebody to take her mother's place and with whom he would be happy.

She had always known that because he was so

attractive he needed a woman to admire him and make a fuss of him.

Reading between the lines of the letter she was sure that was what Lady Bowden was doing.

"Fleur is married," she told herself. "Perhaps Papa will remarry, and that leaves just me unaccounted for!"

She smiled a little wryly and told herself that any idea of her enjoying herself in London and meeting people could now be forgotten.

She was quite certain for one thing that nobody would welcome her because her name was Langford.

The fact that Fleur had run away and married Tim Sheldon who was already engaged to marry the Duke's daughter would be talked about and condemned.

In consequence nobody would wish to entertain Fleur's sister.

She thought that as Cousin Sarah was so angry with Fleur she would undoubtedly ensure that she was branded in the same way that her sister had been.

"I must go home," she told herself. "There is nothing else I can do, and anyway I have no wish to stay in London."

She got up, dressed slowly and asked the old Housemaid to put the clothes that she had brought to London back in the trunk.

Fleur's things that had come with her in the Post-Chaise were still downstairs, and she thought she might as well take them back to the Country as leave them here.

"It will at least save me from having to buy anything new if I want to wear something smart," she decided.

She felt sure that after Fleur had bought new clothes in Paris she would not have any further use for those which had been made in England.

Downstairs Newman told her that there were two horses left in the stable, although the Duke of Hastings had taken his away.

She was relieved that they could take her home drawing the slightly old-fashioned carriage which had not been used, except by Fleur, since her mother had died.

Delysia ordered it to be at the front door at one o'clock and asked Newman if his wife could cook her something to eat before she left.

"You be a'going home, Miss Delysia?" he enquired.

"Yes, Newman. I have had a letter from my father saying that he is feeling better and will soon be leaving Cheltenham, so I must get everything ready for him."

"We'd look after you gladly, if you wants to stay a little longer," Newman said.

Delysia was rather touched by his offer, knowing that after all the extra work that Fleur and Lady Matlock had caused in the house the old couple must be longing for peace and quiet and a chance to rest their legs.

"Perhaps I will come back in a month or so," she replied, "but if I do, I will warn you in plenty of time, so you can engage extra staff to help you."

"Thank you, Miss, that's very kind," Newman replied. "We does our best, but the Missus and me ain't geting any younger."

"I think you have been splendid!" Delysia replied

and knew she had pleased the old man.

She went from the Drawing Room to find that, without the flowers with which it had been decorated when Fleur and Lady Matlock were entertaining, it had lost its glamour.

It was now very obvious that the curtains had faded and some of the chairs needed recovering.

'There is no point in worrying about that, when Fleur is going to have a home of her own,' she thought, 'and Papa never comes to London.'

Then she wondered whether if he married again he might want to bring his new bride here.

She decided that she would discuss the matter with him when he came home and ask if it was worth buying new curtains and having the chairs re-upholstered.

She supposed there were plenty of things with which she could occupy herself. At the same time she still had the feeling that everything had gone flat.

The excitement was over and all she had left was to go back to the lonely life she had spent for the last twelve months since her father had become ill.

"I have often thought that nothing ever happens to me," she murmured.

It seemed incredible that so much in fact, had happened in such a short space of time.

She had travelled to London, been kidnapped, taken by sea to an isolated Castle by a strange, enigmatic man who was determined to keep her a prisoner.

But she had escaped from him and was now, if she was honest, continuing to run away because she was frightened of his anger.

"It is all like a ridiculous tale in a novelette," she said aloud and thought the sound echoed eerily in the empty Drawing Room.

Suddenly the door opened and she heard a man's voice say:

"So you are back! I have called here every day, but nobody seemed to know where you were."

It was Hugo Ludgrove who stood there, looking exceedingly smart with a dazzlingly white cravat at his neck, the points of his collar high above his chin, his Hessian boots shining so brightly they seemed to mirror the furniture as he walked towards her.

"I . . . I returned . . . last night," Delysia said lamely.

"The Butler had no idea what had happened to you," Hugo Ludgrove said. "How could you disappear in that extraordinary fashion? Unless of course, you went with your sister and Tim on their honeymoon!"

"You know they are married?"

"I guessed that Tim intended to elope," he replied. "It was the only thing he could do, and when they suddenly vanished I knew what had happened. But that did not explain why you had gone too."

Delysia, who had no intention of telling him the truth, merely said:

"I am back now, but I am leaving this afternoon for the Country."

"But you cannot do that!"

"Why not?"

"Because I want you to stay here."

She shook her head and said:

"You must realise that would be very unwise when everybody learns that Fleur has married Tim Sheldon."

"They are betting about it in White's Club," Hugo Ludgrove said, "but nobody is certain whether or not it has actually happened."

"Well, it has!" Delysia said. "They were married in Cheltenham, and my father gave Fleur away."

"Good!" Hugo Ludgrove exclaimed with satisfaction. "That is the best possible piece of news! I have known Tim ever since we were at Eton, and I have never known him so much in love."

"That is what I wanted you to say," Delysia smiled, "and although I was a little uncertain before, I feel they will be very happy."

"Of course they will be," Hugo Ludgrove said. "But who is going to look after you?"

His voice had changed as he asked the question and she looked up at him in surprise.

Then when she saw the expression in his eyes she quickly looked away again.

"I know it is too soon," he said in a low voice, "and you will say we do not know each other well enough, but I fell in love with you the moment I saw you!"

Delysia drew in her breath. Then because she felt shy she walked away from him towards the window.

She stood looking out at the sunshine in the small garden that was at the back of the house.

Because there had been nobody living here for so long, the flower-beds had not been planted out with tulips and hyacinths as they had always been in her mother's time.

There were only a few wild daffodils in the beds, and some bushes of lilac and syringa were covered in blossom.

It flashed through Delysia's mind that the garden of the Castle was very much more beautiful.

Then she told herself that was something she had to forget, and it was important that neither Hugo Ludgrove nor anybody else should know where she had been.

She was acutely aware that he was waiting for an answer to what he had just said.

After a moment in a small, rather nervous voice she said:

"I... I do not know you... it is far too... soon to think of... anything like that."

"Well, I am thinking of it," he said in a deep voice. "I have been thinking of it day and night, ever since I first saw you. To tell you the truth, Delysia, you drove me nearly mad by leaving without telling me where you were going."

"I... I am sorry."

"Are you really sorry? I want you to think about me."

She could find nothing to say and after a moment's silence he said:

"You are so absurdly lovely, so beautiful, that I am desperately afraid I shall lose you to the first man who sees you."

Delysia gave him a little smile.

"I am going home," she said, "where there is nobody to see me... except the horses!"

"How can I be sure of that?" Hugo Ludgrove asked. "And if you are leaving London, when shall I see you again?"

"I... I do not... know."

He came a little nearer to her.

"I cannot let you leave like this, when you matter more to me than any other woman I have ever known!"

He drew in his breath before he said:

"I love you, and I intend to make you marry me!"

Delysia turned her head away from him.

"Please . . . you said yourself it is . . . too soon to talk like that . . . and I would not marry anybody unless I was . . . very, very much in love."

She thought as she spoke that she could understand why Fleur had refused so many proposals of marriage before she met Tim.

What she was looking for was what Magnus Fane had called the 'idealists' love' and Fleur had found it.

"That is what I want too!" Delysia told herself.

"If you will only give me a chance, I will make you love me," Hugo Ludgrove said. "I know you are very inexperienced and unsophisticated, but that is why you are so alluring, so exciting. And so, my dear, give me a chance! I swear you will never regret it!"

"It is . . . too soon," Delysia murmured again.

Even as she spoke she knew with a perception that never failed her that, although she liked Hugo Ludgrove, he would never mean anything really important in her life.

She could not explain it, but there was something lacking about him, something which made her know that however nice he was, however pleasant, he would never capture her heart or make her fall in love with him.

Her feelings about it were so strong that she wondered whether she should tell him now that what he was asking was impossible, or whether it would be best to go away and hope he would forget her.

She decided it would be easier to do the latter, and she held out her hand saying:

"I am very honoured and touched that you should say such lovely things to me ... but we have known each other for such a very short time. Perhaps when I come to London again we can meet ... but now I have to return to the Country."

"If you do, I shall follow you," he said, "and I cannot believe you would be so inhospitable as to turn me away from your door."

"That is something I would have to do until my father returns," Delysia replied, "because I shall be living alone at home. But he will be joining me there soon."

"I will try to be patient," he said, "but will you promise me on your honour that when your father has joined you you will invite me to stay?"

He did not wait for her reply but went on:

"In the meantime I am going to tell my mother about you, and I feel sure she would welcome you as a guest either in our country house in Essex, or here in London."

"It is very kind of you," Delysia said. "At the same time you must be aware that, when Fleur and Tim's marriage is publicly announced, there will be quite a number of people, and perhaps your mother amongst them, who will be shocked."

"I know," Hugo Ludgrove agreed, "but personally I am only concerned with you, and whatever anybody else does or says does not interest me."

"I think it does," Delysia contradicted.

"I will come to the Country as soon as you allow me to, and will persuade you that what I have said is true," he said. "In the meantime remember that I love you, and do not lose your heart to any other man."

He raised her hand to his lips as he spoke and his mouth was very gentle against her skin.

It made her remember how rough Magnus Fane had been and the fire of his kisses.

And yet it was strange that although she compared him unfavourably with Hugo Ludgrove, she could not prevent a little quiver from running through her as she remembered the sensations his lips had aroused in her.

She felt instinctively that Hugo Ludgrove was contemplating taking her in his arms.

Hastily she took her hand from his and said:

"Please . . . you must go . . . I am leaving in a very short while, and I have my packing to see to."

"Very well, I will go because you have asked me to," he answered, "but make no mistake, I do not intend to lose you again. If you do not write to me within a few days at White's Club, I will come to the Country. It will not matter if I have to sleep under a hedge or at a Village Inn, just as long as I can be near you."

He spoke with a sudden note of passion in his voice, and reached out to put his arms around her, but Delysia avoided him.

"Goodbye," she said and walked firmly to the open door in case he should prevent her from leaving him.

She ran up the stairs and waited until she knew he left the house before she came down again.

*   *   *

Only when Delysia was driving towards the Country did she reflect that she had just received her first proposal of marriage.

"As Fleur had so many, she would think it strange that this is my first and only one," she told herself with a little smile.

Then she thought that if she could not respond to Hugo Ludgrove as he wanted her to do, it was because, strange though it seemed, she did not care for him.

He was very good-looking, very smartly dressed, and the sort of man whom any woman could be proud to call her husband.

And yet Delysia knew that not for one second had she felt even a flicker of response to the love he had expressed for her.

She knew however ardent he might be, however passionate, it would be impossible for her to give him encouragement to hope that one day she would feel differently.

"Why, why?" she asked herself.

It seemed odd, considering how few men she knew, that when a man had proposed to her she had not found it exciting, or even wanted at least to keep him at her side to enjoy his compliments.

"If I never saw him again, I would not give him a passing thought," she decided.

Sometimes when her father had been more querulous and more difficult than usual during his illness, she had gone to bed imagining there was somebody to comfort her and on whose shoulder she could rest her tired head.

It was a dream which had been part of the Fairy Stories she sometimes told herself to assuage the loneliness of the house where everything centered around a difficult invalid.

'He would love me, and it would be so wonderful to be loved in the way that Papa used to love Mama,' she thought.

But now that a man had actually said he loved her she had not been interested.

It seemed to her so strange that she found herself thinking it over and trying to analyse her feelings.

At the same time it was difficult to think of anybody when her thoughts kept turning to Magnus Fane and wondering what he was thinking and feeling.

Was he furiously angry with her, after his boast that there was no way by which she could escape from the Castle, to find that she had actually managed it?

"I defeated him!" she told herself defiantly, but somehow the words had a hollow ring to them.

She could also hardly believe it, but she felt that frightening though it had been at the Castle, it had been more exciting to be raged at by Magnus Fane and even to be frightened by him, than to be driving alone to an empty house where nobody wanted her.

She knew that when she got there everything would be exactly the same as it had been yesterday, last year, and all the years before that.

'Perhaps I should go back to London, and get to know Hugo Ludgrove better,' Delysia thought.

Then almost as if it was written on her mind in letters of fire, she knew that if there was a choice she would rather return to the Castle and Magnus Fane.

"It is ridiculous!" she said aloud. "I am frightened of him and another time he might not listen to my pleading and . . . make me . . . his."

She was shocked at the very idea and she felt a quiver run through her that seemed to intensify within her breasts until it became a fire.

"I will not think about him!" she declared.

But by the time she reached home she found it impossible not to think about him, and to feel almost as if he was beside her, telling her once again that she could not escape.

The servants were not particularly pleased to see her.

"We thought you'd be away longer than this, Miss Delysia!" the Butler said, "and give us time to do some Spring cleaning in your absence, but we've not got far with it."

"Never mind," Delysia replied. "I expect you have started with the Master's rooms, and as long as they are ready for when he returns, nothing else is of equal importance."

"It's something as 'as to be done," the Butler said reproachfully.

Knowing he expected it, Delysia agreed with him.

She went up to her bedroom, thinking of all that had happened since she had left it to go to London, and that it might be expected she would look older because of everything she had been through.

Instead the face that looked back at her from her mirror seemed very young.

Although she was not so thin or so pale as when she had left, her eyes had a look of bewilderment in them as if she was puzzled by what she saw and did not know what to do about it.

She went to the stables and only when she was with the horses did things seem better.

They at least were glad to see her, and she fed them with tit-bits and talked to them in a soft voice which made them twitch their ears as if they understood.

"I think they are pleased to see me!" she said to the groom.

"Oi be sure they be, Miss Delysia! They misses ye when ye're not 'ere."

"That is what I would like to believe."

But as she walked back to the house, she thought it was not enough. No horse, however wonderful, could fill her life as Tim filled Fleur's.

She ate dinner alone and went to bed feeling very sorry for herself.

She was not at all sure what she wanted, yet she felt like crying until she found it.

Although she slept peacefully, she awoke in the morning feeling unhappy in a way she could not define, only knowing it was there, like an open wound in her heart.

She rode alone, refusing to take a groom with her, and as she jumped the hedges that were so familiar, she found herself thinking of the high one which Magnus Fane had forbidden her to jump.

Then she thought of the way she had fallen off on the other side of it and how angry he had been.

"Why should he have been so angry because I was disobeying him?" she asked.

She knew the answer, and yet it seemed extraordinary that he should mind that she had risked her life or that she should have such an uncontrollable effect on him.

She could feel his whip across her shoulders and the pain his lips had given her.

"I will not remember him, I will not!" she swore.

Yet almost like a ghost walking behind her, he was with her when she went back to the house, when she changed into one of her own simple gowns, and when she went downstairs to the Sitting Room.

It was not decorated with flowers because that had always been one of her tasks when she was at home.

She told herself she ought to go out into the garden and find enough flowers to fill the huge wicker basket which she always carried.

Suddenly she felt it was all too much trouble! Even if she did arrange the flowers who would see them, or care?

"What is the matter with me?" she asked herself aloud.

Even as she heard her voice, which sounded insignificant in the large room, the door opened.

"Mr. Fane, Miss!" the Butler announced.

Because it was so unexpected Delysia turned round with a little cry.

Magnus Fane came into the room, walking with a confidence and assurance which made him seem overwhelming.

And yet as he came towards her she was not frightened, but strangely and inexplicably glad that he was there and she was no longer alone.

It was as if everything lit up and became exciting

again, and she herself had come to life.

He did not hurry towards her, but walked with a kind of deliberation, his eyes on her face.

As she stood waiting for him she felt as if he had come to her across time and space and that they should meet had been ordained by fate.

He reached her and stood looking down at her.

Her eyes were held by his and it was impossible to look away.

There was a long silence before he said:

"I knew I would find you here!"

It was too late now, Delysia thought. It would have been wiser to go to Cheltenham where he would not have thought of looking for her.

And yet somehow she was glad that he had found her, even though it seemed ridiculous that was what she should feel.

"It was clever of you to escape as you did!" he said, "but I suppose you knew I could not let you go!"

"There is . . . no point in your . . . keeping me prisoner . . . now that my . . . sister is . . . m—married."

It was difficult to speak, and somehow her voice sounded very weak and helpless.

"I am aware of that!"

Delysia drew in her breath and went on:

"They are . . . married . . . and they had Papa's permission . . . and he gave Fleur away . . . at the . . . w—wedding."

She meant as she said this to make it sound as if she was confronting him with something he had not expected and that in consequence he would feel he had been defeated.

There was a little silence before Magnus Fane said:

"I have had a letter from my nephew informing me that he and your sister are married, that it is completely legal, and there is nothing I can do to get it annulled."

"Would you want to do anything so...cruel and...unpleasant?" Delysia asked.

"No. Even if there had been some doubt as to its legality, I should have taken no steps in the matter."

She was surprised.

"That is not...what you...intended...originally."

"No, it was not! But I changed my mind or rather you changed it for me."

Delysia had looked away from him, but now she looked up at him in surprise.

"How did I do...that?" she asked a little apprehensively.

"You made me realise that love is more important than anything else!"

"I said that...but you told me that what my sister had for Tim and what he had for her was not the...idealistic love that...some of us sought."

"I know what I said, but as I have already told you, I changed my mind."

"I am...very glad...but why?"

"Because if Fleur is your sister, then I am prepared to believe that she does understand the meaning of idealistic love."

For a moment the significance of what he said did not percolate into Delysia's mind.

Then as she stared at him a little bewildered, she understood, the colour came into her cheeks and she felt herself tremble.

"I suppose you know," Magnus Fane said, "that

you have tortured me unbearably? I hope that never again in the whole of my life will I have to suffer the agonies which exceeded anything endured by a Christian Martyr!"

"I . . . I do not . . . understand!"

The words were only a whisper, and he smiled.

It seemed to transform his face as he said:

"I think you do! You are too intelligent not to realise that when I fell in love with you, I was confronted not only by what I believed were the sins you had committed, but also by the fact that you wanted to marry my nephew."

"You . . . you . . . fell in . . . l–love with me?"

Delysia was not certain if she said the words aloud, or if they were only spoken in her heart.

She only knew that something wild and wonderful was coming alive within her and seeping through her so that it was impossible to think.

She could only feel that Magnus Fane was beside her and in some strange, unaccountable way each could feel the vibrations of the other.

"I could not believe," he went on, "that any woman could look like you, so pure, untouched and innocent, and at the same time have earned a reputation which appalled me!"

"And yet . . . you loved . . . me?"

"I fought against my feelings as I have never fought against anything in my whole life before," he answered. "I told myself I hated and despised you but, just as you told me it would, love triumphed and nothing else was of any importance."

Delysia drew in her breath and her eyes were shining like stars.

Still Magnus Fane did not move, he only said very quietly:

"Now I know, even if you were your sister, even if you had committed every crime in the calendar I should still love you. It is something I cannot prevent, cannot control, and I can only ask you what you intend to do about it."

The deep note in his voice seemed to vibrate through Delysia.

A magical spell seemed to be weaving its way around them, and she felt as if it drew her nearer and nearer to him and she could never escape.

Then with a different note in his voice he said:

"I suppose you want me to apologise, but it was entirely your fault that I believed such things about you, although my instinct told me I was wrong."

"H–how could you believe . . . anything so . . . wicked?" Delysia managed to ask.

"It was what I had been told and what seemed convincing until I actually met you."

He drew in his breath before he asked:

"I should have known that nobody could look so spring-like and perfect, and not be completely innocent."

Suddenly, fiercely, so that her heart seemed to turn a somersault he reached out to hold her by the shoulders and ask:

"It is true—tell me it is true—that no man has ever touched you except me!"

"You know . . . it is . . . true."

She seemed only to breathe the words, but he heard them and asked:

"Have you ever been kissed as I have kissed you?"

She shook her head and saw a light in his eyes that held her spellbound.

"And now what do you intend to do about us?" he asked.

Because her heart was beating wildly so that she felt almost as if it might break out from her breast, she could only answer in a whisper:

"What . . . do you . . . want me to do?"

"I think you know the answer to that," he said, "but I am sure you want it spelled out in words, so I will ask you, Delysia, quite simply, if you will marry me."

As he spoke it seemed to Delysia that the whole room was lit with a light that came from Heaven.

There were no words, nothing she could say to answer him.

Instead, just as she had imagined in her dreams, she moved instinctively forward to hide her face against his shoulder.

Very slowly, it seemed, his arms went round her and as she trembled against him she had the strange feeling that they were joined so irrevocably by some Power greater than themselves that nothing could make them closer than they were already.

Then as if time stood still for them and there was no need to hurry, Magnus Fane put his fingers very gently under her chin and turned her face up to his.

For one moment he looked down at her and she thought she had never seen a man look so happy or so different.

And yet in a way he was god-like, and she was sure there was a celestial light behind him and emanating from him.

Then his lips were on hers.

She knew as he kissed her it was what she had longed for and yearned for although she would not admit it.

Now he was very gentle until as his lips felt the softness of hers his kiss became more insistent, more demanding and more possessive.

He drew her closer and still closer, and as he did so Delysia felt the ecstasy she had known before moving within her.

It was so intense, so glorious, that it seemed to sweep through her like lightning, moving through her breast and up into her throat, then onto her lips.

Linked with him she gave him, as if he had asked for it, her heart and soul.

This was the love she had always known was greater than anything else in the whole world, the love which, as Scott had said, was Heaven.

And she had found it strangely and inexplicably with a man who she had believed hated her.

Only when it seemed as if he took her high into the sky and they touched the burning glory of the sun did she say in a voice that seemed to come from very far away:

"I . . . love you . . . I know now . . . that I . . . I–love you!"

"As I love you, my darling!"

He raised his head to look down at her. Then he said in a voice that did not sound like his own:

"God, how I love you! How can you have done this to me? How can you have given me what I thought I would never find?"

"But you . . . wanted it?"

"Of course I wanted it!" he answered. "But I was sure it existed only in books, poems, music, and the beauty of nature that I saw with my eyes, but which I never thought I would find in my heart."

"I was sure you . . . hated and . . . despised me," Delysia whispered.

"That was how I felt about you until I saw you," he answered. "Then what you call my 'perception' made me know I was mistaken from the very moment we met. You were looking at me in fear, and I knew it was impossible for you to have done any of the things people had accused you of."

"Yet when we were at the Castle . . . you were . . . very angry with me."

Magnus Fane gave a short laugh.

"I was fighting a losing battle, and finding it hard not to believe I had not suddenly gone insane!"

His arms tightened around her as he said:

"I was in love! Wildly, crazily, helplessly in love! But how could I have guessed or even imagined that you would ever love me?"

Because she had to know Delysia said:

"What did you feel when . . . your sister told you that Fleur had . . . married Tim?"

"After the first surprise there was an irrepressible gladness that it was not you!" Magnus Fane replied. "It was not difficult for me to guess, even before my sister had finished telling me what had happened, who you were, but I did not anticipate that you would run away, or that I would go nearly mad in case anything terrible should happen to you on your way to London."

"You . . . knew that was where I had . . . gone?"

"Not until luncheon was announced when I learnt

you were not in the Castle," he said. "It was then my servants informed me of what had happened."

He gave another wry laugh.

"It was clever of you, my darling, but at the same time you should never have thought of journeying all the way to London on your own."

"I was quite . . . safe."

"How was I to know that? I could not sleep for thinking that you might be in danger—not have enough money—or that you might not be accepted at the Inns since you were a woman alone—or worse still, that you might be robbed or injured."

There was so much pain in his voice that Delysia gave a little cry before she said:

"I was quite safe . . . but it is wonderful to know that you were so concerned for . . . my safety. I was thinking . . . just before you came . . . how lonely I was . . . and longing for somebody to . . . look after me and . . . protect me."

She said the last words shyly and Magnus's arms tightened as he replied:

"You will never be able to say that again! You are mine, Delysia, and I will never let you go. I will protect you and look after you for the rest of your life!"

"It all sounds too wonderful to be true! But . . . please . . . I have . . . something to show you."

She moved in his arms and reluctantly he set her free.

She walked across the room to her desk on which lay the letters from Fleur and her father which she had brought downstairs.

She picked Fleur's up.

Then as she turned back to him and saw the way he was looking as he waited, she found it impossible not to run back into the safety of his arms.

He pulled her roughly against him as he had done once before, and said in a voice deep with emotion:

"I cannot lose you, even for a moment. I want you, Delysia! I want you, and now that I have found you, I am desperately afraid I may lose you again."

"You will . . . not do . . . that."

"Then how soon will you marry me?"

"Whenever you . . . want me to."

He laughed.

"Oh, my darling, you always say the unexpected. I feel that any other woman would first have considered whether she had anything to wear, or how unconventional she was being."

The last words were lost against Delysia's lips, and he kissed her until she felt as if the room was spinning dizzily around them and once again they were floating up into the sky.

Only when it was possible to speak again did she say:

"Please . . . before we talk of marriage . . . I want you to read this letter."

"I will read anything you like, but I have already decided that I cannot wait any longer for you," Magnus Fane said. "I obtained a Special Licence on my way through London, otherwise I would have been here yesterday!"

He would have kissed her again, but Delysia pressed Fleur's letter into his hand.

Although she felt he resented his attention being diverted from her, he brought it up to eye-level, at the same time holding her tightly against him with his other arm.

Delysia put her head against his shoulder as he read it, thinking that everything was perfect.

But she could not let Magnus go on thinking that her sister had done all the despicable things he had been told she had.

'Now he will understand,' she thought.

She could feel his heart beating against hers and she knew she loved him and nobody else in the whole world could mean anything to her.

She supposed if they had not met she might have considered Hugo Ludgrove as a husband, simply because he was suitable, and she was sure he had a very pleasant character.

If he loved a woman, she told herself, he would make her happy.

But as far as she was concerned, she could never have given him the idealistic love in which she believed and which she knew now Magnus had for her, and she for him.

It was love that Scott understood and which, as Magnus had said, everybody sought, although many were disappointed.

He read the letter. Then he asked:

"Do you forgive me?"

"For thinking all those things about Fleur? You know now they are . . . not true."

"I knew it before," he said. "Loving you as I do has convinced me that your sister could never do anything really bad, because she has been brought up with the same ideals and outlook as yourself."

"Thank you," Delysia said softly. "That is a wonderful thing to say, and I know Mama would have been very, very proud."

"I not only think it, I believe it because I believe in you," Magnus replied. "Oh, my darling, how can you be so perfect in every way? You are, although I would never admit it to anybody else, what I dreamed of in my secret heart."

"As . . . I dreamed of you," Delysia said. "The man I turned to for . . . protection and love had no . . . face. Now I know it was you and that fate in the strangest way, has brought us together."

"If fate had not done it in this way, it would have happened in another," Magnus said. "I believe my own destiny has brought me half-way across the world to find you."

"And to think I nearly . . . escaped from . . . you."

"Only so that I could find you again. There is no hiding-place for us from each other, either amongst the stars or in the depths of the ocean. You are mine, Delysia! Mine, now and for all eternity!"

Once again he was kissing her, and his kisses gave her a love that was so perfect, so divine that she could only feel her whole body respond.

He raised his head and looked down at her with an expression of love which transformed his face.

Then he asked with a faint smile:

"Am I still the 'Demon King'?"

Delysia gave a little laugh.

"Certainly a King," she said. "Awe-inspiring and a little frightening. At the same time so unusual that I am still afraid you will suddenly disappear."

"It was you who did that!" he replied. "But I will make certain that you never want to do so again!"

He spoke with the same air of authority, the same possessive firmness which Delysia loved, because it was so essentially him that she could not imagine him any other way.

She knew that whatever happened in the future, he would always be her Master, the man she would instinctively obey, the man she would look up to and admire.

At the same time, he would protect her, look after her, and never again would she be lonely or afraid.

He was watching her eyes and reading her thoughts.

"You are mine," he said, "and we have a million exciting things to do together! But I warn you, my precious, I shall be a very jealous husband!"

Delysia gave a little laugh.

"If there are any other men in the world," she said, "I shall not be aware of them."

"I will take care of that," Magnus said almost angrily, "and if you so much as flirt with any of them, I promise I will take you back to the Castle and lock you up until you are as penitent as I meant you to be when I took you aboard my yacht."

Delysia pressed herself closer to him.

"I was . . . prepared to be . . . penitent."

"Nonsense!" he answered. "You set out to intrigue, bewilder and bemuse me until I could see nothing but your eyes and feel drawn towards you by a magic spell from which I could not escape."

Delysia gave a cry of delight.

"Why did you not . . . tell me . . . that?"

"I tried to show you what I felt in a rather different way."

She knew he was thinking of how he had come to her room, thrown her on the bed and intended to make her his.

The colour flooded into her cheeks as she hid her face against his shoulder.

"I can only say that I am sorry," Magnus Fane said softly, "but I wanted you so desperately and I had forced myself to believe all the things I had been told about you."

"You do know now that neither Fleur nor I would ever do . . . anything so wrong . . . so wicked?"

Magnus's arms tightened so that it was difficult for her to breathe.

"I adore you," he said, "and while as a woman you excite me wildly and uncontrollably, I worship you as something so perfect that you are the only woman I have ever met in my whole life whom I have wanted to be the mother of my children."

Delysia lifted her face to his.

"That is a very beautiful thing to say to me."

"I mean it," he said, "and when we are married, my adorable one, I will make love to you in a very different way from how I behaved the other night at the Castle."

As he spoke Delysia saw the fire come into his eyes and as hers dropped before his she said, so softly that he could only just hear her:

"I know that it will be very . . . wonderful and also very . . . exciting!"

"I promise you that because we love each other and because I love you more than any woman has ever been loved before, it will be the Heaven Scott spoke of and which you, my darling, have convinced me really exists."

"Did I really do . . . that?"

"We have just reached the gates of Heaven," Magnus replied. "After we are married we will go inside them."

His lips were almost touching hers as he asked:

"Why are we wasting time? Let us get married, my lovely, and I will admit that you were completely and absolutely right: Love is Heaven and Heaven is Love."

ABOUT THE AUTHOR

Barbara Cartland, the world's most famous romantic novelist, who is also an historian, playwright, lecturer, political speaker and television personality, has now written over 370 books and sold over 370 million books the world over.

She has also had many historical works published and has written four autobiographies as well as the biographies of her mother and that of her brother, Ronald Cartland, who was the first Member of Parliament to be killed in the last war. This book has a preface by Sir Winston Churchill and has just been republished with an introduction by Sir Arthur Bryant.

Love at the Helm, a novel written with the help and inspiration of the late Admiral of the Fleet, the Earl Mountbatten of Burma, is being sold for the Mountbatten Memorial Trust.

Miss Cartland in 1978 sang an Album of Love Songs with the Royal Philharmonic Orchestra.

In 1976 by writing twenty-one books, she broke the world record and has continued for the following seven years with twenty-four, twenty, twenty-three, twenty-four, twenty-four, twenty-five, and twenty-three. She is in the *Guinness Book of Records* as the best-selling author in the world.

She is unique in that she was one and two in the Dalton List of Best Sellers, and one week had four books in the top twenty.

In private life Barbara Cartland, who is a Dame of the Order of St. John of Jerusalem, Chairman of the St. John Council in Hertfordshire and Deputy President of the St. John Ambulance Brigade, has also fought for better conditions and salaries for Midwives and Nurses.

Barbara Cartland is deeply interested in Vitamin Therapy and is President of the British National Association for Health. Her book *The Magic of Honey* has sold throughout the world and is translated into many languages. Her designs "Decorating with Love" are being sold all over the U.S.A., and the National Home Fashions League named her in 1981, "Woman of Achievement."

Barbara Cartland's Romances (a book of cartoons) has recently been published in Great Britain and the U.S.A., as well as *Getting Older, Growing Younger*, and a cookery book, *The Romance of Food*.

More romance from

BARBARA CARTLAND

__07308-3	BRIDE TO A BRIGAND #7	$2.50
__07607-4	LOVE COMES WEST #8	$2.50
__07649-X	THE STORMS OF LOVE #11	$2.50
__07732-1	MOONLIGHT ON THE SPHINX #12	$2.50
__07745-3	WHITE LILAC #13	$2.50
__07879-4	REVENGE OF THE HEART #14	$2.50
__07911-1	THE ISLAND OF LOVE #15	$2.50
__08053-3	THERESA AND A TIGER #16	$2.50
__08079-9	LOVE IS HEAVEN #17	$2.50

Prices may be slightly higher in Canada.

Available at your local bookstore or return this form to:

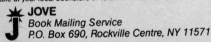

JOVE
Book Mailing Service
P.O. Box 690, Rockville Centre, NY 11571

Please send me the titles checked above. I enclose _____. Include 75¢ for postage and handling if one book is ordered; 25¢ per book for two or more not to exceed $1.75. California, Illinois, New York and Tennessee residents please add sales tax.

NAME_____

ADDRESS_____

CITY_____ STATE/ZIP_____

(allow six weeks for delivery)

BARBARA CARTLAND

Called after her own
beloved Camfield Place,
each Camfield novel of love
by Barbara Cartland
is a thrilling, never-before published
love story by the greatest romance
writer of all time.

February...MIRACLE FOR A MADONNA
March...A VERY UNUSUAL WIFE
April...THE PERIL AND THE PRINCE